The Original
Edison Field

The Original Edison Field

THE SUMMER OF '51 INSPIRES
THE DREAMS OF A 10-YEAR-OLD BOY

Homer Wallop

iUniverse, Inc.
Bloomington

THE ORIGINAL EDISON FIELD
THE SUMMER OF '51 INSPIRES THE DREAMS OF A 10-YEAR-OLD BOY

iUniverse books may be ordered through booksellers or by contacting:

iUniverse
1663 Liberty Drive
Bloomington, IN 47403
www.iuniverse.com
1-800-Authors (1-800-288-4677)

Front cover design: jgimages
Back cover design: jgimages
Photo of Bobby Thomson: jgimages

ISBN: 978-1-4759-6284-0 (sc)
ISBN: 978-1-4759-6285-7 (ebk)

Library of Congress Control Number: 2012921699

Printed in the United States of America

iUniverse rev. date: 11/19/2012

Prologue

This story about the life of Jimmy Fletcher and baseball begins long before the Los Angeles Angels (the major league version) were created in 1961 and later moved to Anaheim and became the California Angels. It begins long before the Big A was built and the stadium later was saddled for a short time with the corporately unwieldy name of Edison International Field of Anaheim. It begins long ago in the heartland of California, far from the din of the big cities, where a small front yard on Edison Street in the fictional town of Marshfield became Jimmy's refuge from the pain of his parents' divorce. Jimmy and his closest buddies transformed their special ball field into The Original Edison Field. Of course, neither they nor Jimmy called it that at the time. What concerned him more was playing baseball as if hardly anything else mattered and coping with some hard lessons as he went along in life. The season of 1951 was only the beginning.

Part One

1951 was a year that sticks as only it could in the mind of a 10-year-old boy.

The summer was bright and green and hot, and a relief from the cauldron of fog and dark winters that fill the Central Valley of California and, more to the point, Jimmy Fletcher's first new-found hard edges of life. He stumbled onto them by accident, as if slicing your finger on a rusty razor blade lurking at the bottom of a box of junk. From out of nowhere, they came down on him heavily, unexpected, unwanted. It was the first summer after Jimmy's parents divorced and Norman contracted polio.

Before that summer arrived, go back six months when the tule fog was so thick you couldn't see as far as the hood ornament on your car. It was downright depressing, and, while everybody was trying cheerfully to usher in a new year, the year was beginning in its usual, foreboding manner, Jimmy thought when he was much older. Christmas vacation was winding down, and soon he would again be riding his Schwinn bicycle, called a Black Panther model, even if it was red, through the duck soup four blocks to school.

But that would happen on Tuesday, January the second, 1951, and it was only Friday night, and Jimmy and his mother were sitting in the living room of their two-bedroom house on Edison Street in Marshfield.

"Where's Daddy?" he asked.

"He's out in the garage," she answered, not giving a hint of what was to come. "Go see him."

Jimmy ran outside and into the garage.

"What are you doing?" he asked eagerly.

"I am putting new license plates on the car," his father said.

"Why are you doing it tonight?" Jimmy asked. Knowing that everybody in the state received new plates for the new year, he didn't think it strange, but why tonight?

"We are going to Oakville tomorrow," he said.

Jimmy was thrilled with the idea because that's the town where he was born and where they lived until he was 5. Though it was during World War Two, for Jimmy the memories were pleasant and sweet—and he was perfectly contented when he demanded—and got his way—to wear 100 percent wool sailor suits, despite the fact that everybody else was sweltering in the heat.

"But why are we going?" he prodded.

"Go ask your mother." It was as much an answer as it was a command.

His mother was still in the same position when Jimmy returned, as if frozen in time. Only now she was crying. She gave Jimmy the stark news—they were getting a divorce, and Jimmy would live with his father. It was simply easier that way, and that was that. Now he was sobbing along with her.

Sure enough, the next day they left for Oakville and moved his mother into the one-bedroom house his dad somehow was able to build right before the war when the Great Depression was hanging around like the tule fog, and which his parents still owned. She didn't have many possessions, so it didn't take much time to get her settled.

Too soon it was time to leave Oakville, and Jimmy started sniffling again. Making one last inspection of the one-car garage, his dad found an Army bayonet. It had 1901 stamped near the hilt. Nobody knew whether it was made that year or whether it had killed anybody in World War One or World War Two. So, his father gave it to him, trying to make peace, Jimmy supposed much later. Maybe it was all he could think to do.

Then, the two of them got back into the 1948 Ford sedan. Jimmy was so distraught that he couldn't even remember saying goodbye to his mother. The car pulled away and was on the two-lane highway back to Marshfield. The tears came again in torrents, and he couldn't stop crying.

"That's enough," his father said sharply. Jimmy always did what he was told, and stopped.

Secretly, Jimmy cried all the time, but his father never saw him cry and never knew. He did well in school, but he was angry and got into a fight once with a classmate who had reason to be angrier than Jimmy. His classmate's mother died when they were only 8, in the third grade.

Jimmy would see his mother only on school vacations after that.

★ ★ ★

Mainly, Jimmy pushed his anger inside, and he couldn't say the word "divorce" for several years. On the outside, he appeared happy and he must have heard somewhere about hope springing eternal, and all that dreamy mush. He dreamed only of his mother. Well, with the exception of one other dream he had—to play for the Yankees, his favorite team, especially when they were winning, and it seemed they always were.

There was no mistaking he loved baseball. Somehow it became a part of him, almost instantly, magically, when he first heard the names of Joe DiMaggio and Jackie Robinson and Ted Williams and Bob Feller not long after the war ended. Maybe he had an inkling they were baseball players, but their teams? He couldn't have told you, though he soon learned.

The Cleveland Indians won the World Series in 1948, but Jimmy took the Yankees into his heart, and the 1949 season was the first he followed from start to finish. As far as he was concerned, the Indians and the Red Sox were teams that only annoyed the Yankees like a pesky fly. Why worry about the Dodgers? They were in the other league, and besides, they never won the World Series anyway. They were always being beaten by the Yankees.

Some of his pals were baseball fans, too, but never Yankee fans. As far as he knew, nobody else in Marshfield ever liked the Yankees—in fact, hated them is a better description. That didn't seem to matter to three of his closest buddies because they always played together, just as it didn't matter that Dominic and Ronnie were two years older, or that Duane, also Jimmy's age, was convinced by his older brothers that he could fly like Superman and once launched himself from a branch in the English walnut tree across Edison street.

Jimmy would say all of them lived on his block, but their street was just one long skinny street, more like a country road, and paved with more flattened dead toads than black top. The toads came out in the muggy summer nights, and passing cars splattered them like cow pies. The boys lived three blocks beyond the city limit sign, so it was almost out in the country, but no county road crew ever came to pry up the dried, flattened toads and cart them off.

It was during Easter vacation, in March that year, when they met Norman, on one of those miserable days that are caught between winter and spring. Opening Day for the big leagues was almost four weeks away, and they hadn't played catch since the 1950 season ended. The foul weather and wet grass were not going to deny them. Norman must have seen them through his window, and he came out of the bleach-white clapboard house next door. Because they weren't watching too closely, nobody saw how he negotiated off the porch and down the concrete steps. He wasn't in a wheelchair, but in a strange-looking walker with four wheels and a seat he could use if, Jimmy thought, he got tired.

"Hi, fellas," he said. "I saw you playing and thought I'd come out for a while. I used to play baseball and even some football, but not now."

Norman had polio. Sometimes it was called infantile paralysis, and there always was a campaign to raise money to wipe it out. For Norman, there was nothing infantile about it. He had contracted the dreaded disease a full year earlier, in 1950, when he was 15. So the spring of 1951 was a new beginning for Norman, too. He could walk if he put on braces that went from his waist to the bottoms of his shoes. But walking in the braces was difficult, and he had to bend sideways with each step. The walker made it a lot easier for him to get around.

He told them a little about this disease and said he was in an iron lung at first.

"What's an iron lung?" they asked, almost in unison.

He wasn't offended and explained, "It's a round machine like a large tube, and I had to lay in it so I could breathe. If I didn't use it for a while, my lungs would not work, and I'd die."

"Gee," Jimmy said, "are you OK now?"

"Yes, my lungs slowly got better, but the polio left my legs paralyzed. So I can't play baseball any more. And for sure not football."

Dominic asked, "Where did you play? In college?" Even to a bunch of kids, they could see that Norman was a lot older than them. He was four whole years older than Dominic and Ronnie.

"Only in high school," Norman said. "I was our team's starting catcher."

"Well," Ronnie said, "how did you get polio?"

"My mother says it was because I played football," Norman said, "but who knows?"

At that instant, his mother, Evelyn, stomped out onto the porch and, in her penetrating voice, answered Norman's question herself, not that he wanted an answer. He would have simply liked an answer that would let him run and play again.

She hollered, "He got it from playing football. You kids, you make sure you never play football. You'll get polio, just like my Norman. He was a star player at Monte Vista High, but now look at him." Then, she turned on her heels and disappeared inside.

His mother had remarried, so Norman had a second father. But Charlie was a cold and distant man in Norman's life. Charlie worked as a supervisor at the local cannery, and the pressure to fill government contracts for peaches canned in heavy syrup was almost unbearable. Charlie's standing order to Evelyn was to have a tall glass of Scotch whisky waiting when he came through the door.

Because Norman lived with them just during school vacations, he was affected by Charlie's indifference only in a shallow way, or so it seemed. The truth was, it compounded the deep hurt already in Norman's life, for it wasn't the first tragedy he had known. His real father, Andy, left for the Army early in 1942 when Norman was but 7 years old. Before Andy was shipped out to the Pacific Theater, he came home on a weekend furlough, and Norman clearly remembered what his father told him as he said goodbye: "I'll be coming back soon, and we'll play catch then." It was the last time Norman saw him. Although Andy somehow survived the brutality of the Bataan Death March through the tropical Philippine jungle, he wasted away with dysentery in the prisoner of war camp afterward.

Then came the tragedy of polio eight years later. Norman was tall, if you asked Jimmy or Ronnie or Dominic, but only about 5 feet, 8 inches. He had a solid build, and his coach in his freshman year determined Norman was the perfect size to play catcher. Halfway through his sophomore year, Norman was struck with the polio. He spent long hours lying flat on his back in that iron lung and was visible only from the bottom of his chin up. Norman had black, curly hair, and it was easy to see he was a good-looking kid. His first and only girlfriend came to visit him at his mother's house once, and they could only look at each other through the mirror mounted on the end of the iron lung's tube. She cried at the sight of Norman. He could speak only in whispers, and it was so difficult for her that she never came again. After seven months of the iron lung and other rehabilitation, Norman, luckier than many, regained use of his upper body and could breathe freely again, and throw a baseball.

* * *

"Is it OK," Norman said, "if I play some catch with you? I can still throw. Well, I think I can." It was his arm's first test in more than a year.

"Sure," they answered, again together. "Do you have a mitt?"

"Not here. I have two at my uncle's apartment, a first base mitt and a catcher's mitt. I live with him." He didn't feel like telling them about his real father, or that it was easier than living around Charlie.

Jimmy said, "We have only our gloves, so we'll make sure we throw easy so you can catch with just your bare hands until you bring one of yours."

"OK, and I can sit down in my walker."

After a while, even a game of catch gets boring, and they looked for something new to do.

Norman already had seen Jimmy's baseball bat lying on the sidewalk in front of his porch with the concrete steps.

He said, "Let's play a game."

They looked at each other, afraid to say anything, because how could he swing a bat in that walker or run if he did hit the ball? How could he play a game of workups? So what did he mean? He was thinking far ahead of them.

"I'll make up a game," he said. As they soon learned, Norman knew all the rules of baseball, and he taught them all of the fine points. And he made all the rules for their little field, Jimmy's front yard on Edison Street in Marshfield.

Theirs was a game of simplicity, and here's how Norman laid out all the rules:

There were two young magnolia trees, thin and not very tall, and equidistant apart, about 15 feet from the steps of the front porch, right where home plate would be.

Norman said, "The left and right foul lines will be those trees. If a batted ball hits the trunks, it's an automatic base hit. Catch a ground ball before it stops rolling, and the batter is out. There is no bunting, and a ball has to travel past that first crack across the sidewalk."

The sidewalk with a single S-curve to straightaway center field led to a gap in the hedge that separated the lawn and the one-lane Edison Street. Hit the hedge—maybe all of 55 feet away—on the fly, and you had a double. Oddly, Norman made no proviso for triples.

They couldn't swing for the fences. Norman made sure of that. Hit one over the hedge, and there were two penalties. One, you were out, and, two, you had to chase the ball, oftentimes digging it out of a tangled honeysuckle bush. Or, worse, across Edison into the cow pasture.

The only bat they had was Jimmy's 28-inch-long model, and the handle eventually became chipped and the knob disappeared. Jimmy's glove was a replica of the Rawlings model he saw at the sporting goods store. It was a three-finger model called "Playmaker," and had Marty Marion's name embossed on it, though it came from the Montgomery Ward's catalog. They played so often that they frequently had to replace the 10-inch ball when they knocked off its rubber cover. If it split apart in the middle of a tense game—for example, the Yankees vs. the Red Sox—they used some friction tape to wrap around it. If they had the time and could put enough money together, they'd ride their bicycles five blocks to the sporting goods store for a new ball. The sporting goods store always had a strange smell, a combination of glove leather and sturgeon brought in from down in San Pablo Bay.

Norman's game taught them how to hit up the middle of a baseball diamond. The safest place, the most unprotected place, Norman told them, was to center. There was a priceless premium on that principle: The only way to hit a home run was directly through the gap in the hedge, the width of the sidewalk. They named it "Home Run Alley."

And hit ground balls. They were tougher to field, especially on the lumpy grass with the high edge along the S-shaped sidewalk. Besides, a line drive was just like playing catch. Anybody could do it.

There were plenty of foul balls straight back, and the screen door "backstop" took a beating. Jimmy's father didn't seem to mind, and he could be a stickler, and certainly never a baseball fan. His name was on the roster, unofficial of course, of the town's Yankee-haters, and he nicknamed them "the Jerkees," just to needle Jimmy. But he never said a word when they wore a bald spot in the lawn where the "mound" was, when Norman wasn't there to pitch to them.

Because there were no bases to run, they only ran for cover—when a foul ball would pop over the front gable and down the east slope of the roof into Evelyn's driveway and up against the side of her house. She would charge out and stand on her porch, screaming at them—"You noisy, unruly brats."

Always quick of foot and quick of mind, Ronnie shouted back: "We have our rules, so how can we be un-RULE-y?" He laughed and laughed, infuriating Evelyn all the more, and she stomped back into her house. Jimmy's father called her "neurotic," a term as foreign to him then as "alcoholic," which she probably was.

Through the summer, Norman sat in his walker and pitched to them—right-handed or left-handed—he was that talented—as they conducted their vicarious pennant races.

Jimmy always represented his heroes of the day—Rizzuto, Raschi, Berra and DiMaggio. It was DiMaggio's final season, and Mickey Mantle, a struggling rookie, was waiting in the wings, in right field, to be exact. Jimmy had the same fresh-faced look, toothy grin and blond hair just like Mantle's.

Dominic was from the Providence area, not far from Boston. At least that's where he lived before. That's why his lineup was made up of his Red Sox heroes—Goodman, Williams, Dom

9

DiMaggio and Dropo, and Ellis Kinder or Mel Parnell or Mickey McDermott on the mound. Maybe he was born in Rhode Island, but certainly his family came to live in the Central Valley as did many Portuguese dairy farmers from the Azores islands.

The boys batted left or right, mimicking their favorites to their imaginations' content. Once in a while, they played as if they were Stan Musial and copied his corkscrew batting stance.

Arriving daily was the pressure they always savored. Bases loaded, two men out, a full count, the bottom of the ninth, seventh game of the World Series.

Jimmy and his best friends—Dominic, Ronnie, Duane and Norman—made that tiny patch of grass come alive, grander than the angular fence lines of the Polo Grounds or the band-box dimensions of Ebbets Field or expansive Yankee Stadium. It was Jimmy's ball yard and refuge and his early proving ground for his dream of reaching the big leagues. "I'll get there someday," he liked to say.

Jimmy was never without the mail-order New York Yankee baseball cap he found advertised in a sports magazine. The cap cost $3. Postage was extra. He didn't have the money right away, but Evelyn hired him to mow her front lawn each week. She paid him 50 cents a week, so six weeks later he sent away for the cap. It took forever to arrive, at least in his mind. It was deep navy blue, and looked authentic, but it wasn't. The white NY on it was cut out of felt probably on somebody's kitchen table and stitched with a single thread. Years later, Jimmy took it out of his closet to look at it. "What a piece of junk," he thought. But he wore it everywhere he went until he outgrew it. It certainly lasted longer than the red and yellow cap he bought at the local five-and-ten store. That cap cost only a dime. It was always on his head until the wind blew it off when he and Dominic were sitting on the top of the fence of a neighbor's pig sty. It was inadvisable to step into the sty to retrieve it, and it was already too late. The pigs ate it.

The "Yankee" cap provided some shade, and, as hot as that summer was, the pennant races were hotter. The Yankees and Red Sox were fighting for first place in the American League. The Giants were languishing in second place behind the Dodgers in the National League. And the season had not reached the halfway point. It was only June 30. The All-Star Game was still two weeks away.

The game the day before was a telling clue to the season. The Yankees and Red Sox—a fever-pitch rivalry—were holding nothing back. Baseball's top money players were going head to head in a classic battle: Right-hander Vic Raschi vs. southpaw Mickey McDermott on the mound, Joe DiMaggio vs. Ted Williams at the plate.

Williams had not lost any of his intensity for the game, though it was exactly 10 years after he hit .406. Through those kids, without ever knowing it, he brought all of his mastery of hitting a baseball to 406 E. Edison St. Jimmy wondered, "Why couldn't my house be at 56 E. Edison, and then I could brag that I would always have a connection to DiMaggio and his 56-game hitting streak? Just like Dominic brags about Williams and his hitting?" DiMaggio's magical streak also happened 10 years earlier.

Nearly every day, they reenacted the previous day's box scores, and this day was no different. If they didn't remember what each player had done, they kept a copy of the box score handy, clipped from the local afternoon paper.

Norman was pitching in his walker alongside the bushy evergreen shrub, and Dominic was in left field. Nobody knew where Ronnie or Duane was. Maybe Duane's brothers had sent him on another sortie from a tree.

Though they knew the outcome of the game, they always played it straight, and they had to hit for themselves. Boston/

Williams/Dominic drew first blood in the fourth inning, driving in Johnny Pesky with a single to right, 1-0.

If the Yankee lineup was usually powerful, it wasn't quite so this year. Gil McDougald was the only regular player batting over .300. He finished at .301, to be exact—good enough to earn rookie-of-the-year honors.

In the fifth inning, the Yankees mounted a rally as Hank Bauer led off with a double and Jackie Jensen walked. McDougald settled into the batter's box with his strange-looking stance of holding his bat straight back, parallel to the ground. McDougald promptly singled to left, tying the score, 1-1.

McDermott retired the next nine Yankees. Raschi matched him, also facing only nine batters through the sixth, seventh and eighth innings.

With McDermott still throwing flames and apparently on automatic pilot, the bottom of the eighth was at hand and the tension mounting. And Norman was mimicking him, throwing left-handed. Jimmy was at the plate batting left or right, according to which Yankee was at bat.

Pitcher Raschi was the leadoff batter and unlikely to do any damage. His batting average was a lofty .143. He promptly singled to right field. Surprisingly, manager Casey Stengel did not send in a runner for Raschi. Phil Rizzuto singled to left and moved to second base after a force out. With two outs, DiMaggio/Jimmy was next.

Jimmy, Dominic and Norman pretended they could hear the public address announcer as DiMaggio approached the batter's box. They had no idea what the public address announcer really said because the radio broadcasts were not live, but were re-created by Liberty Broadcasting System, probably in some secret studio somewhere. Still, they imagined the announcer's God-like voice might have reverberated like this in cavernous Yankee Stadium: **Now** batting, batting, batting **Number** Five Five Five **Joe** DiMaggio DiMaggio DiMaggio.

Then came the pitch of the game from Norman.

DiMaggio—that is, Jimmy—ripped a line drive to right centerfield, buzzing over Norman's head and sticking in the hedge for a double. Rizzuto, blessed with quickness—that's why he was called "Scooter," easily scored the go-ahead run. So, the Yankees held a tenuous 2-1 lead, and the only part left was for Raschi—that is, Norman—to close out the victory in the top of the ninth inning, and he did for Raschi's 12th win against four losses.

Dominic couldn't help but feel defeated, even in their make-believe stadium. But that's how the season went, and they couldn't rewrite a single line in the box scores. Even though they represented their rival teams, they were friends enough to leave that rivalry on the field when the game was over and they went on to other important things for boys to do in the blazing hot summer.

"Hey," Jimmy said, in an attempt to make Dominic forget his team lost, "let's go swimming."

Dominic said, "Well, we gotta go check and see if the ditch is in."

An irrigation ditch ran right behind Jimmy's house, and some of it was lined with concrete and then an underground pipe, 20 feet long, where the terrain dropped about 10 feet. Someone once challenged Ronnie to hold his breath and swim through it. He made it, but Jimmy never tried. He knew there was a chain across the inside of the pipe, about in the middle, and he was afraid he'd get hung up on it and be found with only some shreds of meat hanging off his bones next winter when there was no water in the ditch. Where the pipe ended was their favorite swimming hole, a wide place where back eddies and a pool formed. Two rows of tall cottonwood trees stood on each side, and a sandy beach was a few yards downstream.

Jimmy often swam there alone, and the only time he was frightened was when something as large and as hard as an enormous chunk of concrete bumped him from behind. A young calf had drowned, and the carcass bobbed up out of the culvert. The dead calf had no problem making it past the chained pipe. Chills went up Jimmy's back, and it was like he sprouted wings and seemingly flew out of the ditch. He didn't tell anyone about the calf, figuring their swimming hole would be declared off-limits by his father. Or by Evelyn. Indeed, her other warning haunted him at that moment: "You'll get polio swimming in that irrigation ditch. There are polio germs in that water." He forgot her words as soon as he reached the safety of his house, and the panic was gone. He never got polio.

So, Jimmy and Dominic ran through his back yard to see whether the ditch had water. It was empty. Down deep, Jimmy was happy because he still had pictures of that calf in his mind. Dominic continued to sulk a little, but had another idea. "Let's go see if Brown's ditch is in," he said. "If this one isn't in, the other might be. They alternate the irrigation schedules. That's the way they do it."

"Well, if you say so," Jimmy said without any real enthusiasm. They hopped on Jimmy's bicycle and he pumped Dominic on the handle bars, and they rode as quickly as they could six blocks, almost to downtown, to Brown's ditch, which also had a wide place where a pool formed. They were in luck. The ditch was full.

Already there were Duane—he had survived his latest sortie—his brothers Lonnie and Leroy, and their cousin, Lenny, and some of the oldest boys' friends. Dominic and Jimmy jumped in.

Unknown to Jimmy, the middle of the pool was very deep, and suddenly the bottom fell out from under him. It took him by surprise, and he took in a mouthful of water and couldn't find the sand with his feet. He came to the surface once but was ready to go under a second time. He could swim OK, but he wasn't a strong swimmer. He weighed only 40 pounds. No one was watching him except Dominic. He dived in and grabbed Jimmy and hauled him to the sandy bank.

Dominic said, "Well, maybe we've had enough swimming for today. Let's go home." Jimmy was thankful and relieved. He didn't say a word, and he couldn't remember ever thanking Dominic for saving his life. Of course, Dominic probably knew how embarrassed Jimmy was.

One day in July, Ronnie and Jimmy rode their bicycles to downtown Marshfield. Dominic said he had something to do at home. He probably made up an excuse because he didn't own a bike, and, for some reason, no one offered to pump him. And Duane? He told them he needed to make a cape with a big red S on it. There was a new store downtown that Ronnie and Jimmy had discovered, and wanted to see. It wasn't too hard to find, right on the other side of the railroad tracks. The store was called The Browse Shop, and they could read comic books and their favorite sports magazines until they were told to buy.

They pulled a copy of *Sport* magazine off the rack. It had a picture on the cover of Ewell "The Whip" Blackwell. While he wasn't one of their true heroes, he was a famous baseball player and had pitched a no-hitter for the Cincinnati Reds. One article was trumpeted on the cover: "Can Boudreau help the Red Sox do it?"

"Are you kidding?" Jimmy said, answering that question with a question that settled the entire matter. It was a good thing that Dominic wasn't with them. He might have punched Jimmy in the nose, or let him drown, given a second chance.

When the clerk made it clear it was time to buy or leave—"This isn't a library, you know," the woman said stiffly—they pooled 25 cents, all nickels and pennies, for the magazine. Going out the door, Ronnie cracked, "I thought it was called 'The Browse Shop'?" As fast as they could get away, they rode home and never again darkened the door of The Browse Shop.

Back at Ronnie's house, the magazine captured their imaginations even better than the box scores. They told Dominic about their treasure, and all of them showed up the next morning, again at Ronnie's house. Duane lived next door and came over. He had a goose egg on his forehead.

Ronnie's parents worked, and the boys had the house to themselves. They generally sprawled all over the couch, the easy chair and even the floor, or they huddled around the radio and listened to Gordon "The Old Scotchman" McLendon or Al Helfer announce a game.

This day, they had no plan in particular, other than to laze around, pore through the magazine, see who could chew and spit sunflower seeds the fastest, and talk about baseball, swimming and other important topics.

Dominic said, "You hear about the Giant player who was laying on a woman?"

Jimmy said, "What was he doing laying on a woman?"

"Ah, c'mon," Ronnie said, "you know."

"No, I don't," Jimmy protested.

"Well, then," Dominic said, "you're too young to find out. So, I'm telling you, he was so big, he killed her."

"No, he didn't," Ronnie said. "He wasn't that big."

"Well," Dominic said, "he was a Giant, and maybe he was giant."

The two older boys who knew what was up laughed out loud, and it was Jimmy's first clue about male and female relationships, though he still didn't quite get it. But he'd be switched if anyone was going to convince him that his Sunday school teacher had ever been in such a gross position.

Jimmy believed strongly in God and went to church every Sunday morning and evening, and even to Wednesday night prayer meetings, because Mrs. Lance came and gave him a lift religiously. She would have picked him up on Saturday nights, too, if the church doors had been open.

"No, not Mrs. Lance," Jimmy protested. "She wouldn't do anything like that. She's a church-going lady." She had four children.

The other two boys just shook their heads as Ronnie changed the subject.

"OK, what did the Yankees do yesterday?" Ronnie asked.

"You know what they did," Jimmy said. "Didn't Dominic tell you we played the game?"

"Yeah, he said something," Ronnie said, "but not much."

"Well, why should I? It wasn't much fun," Dominic said.

Jimmy said, "It will be fun when I grow up and play for the Yankees. That's all I want to do when I get big."

Duane was certain what he *didn't want* to do. He said, "I don't want to learn how to play the guitar. My mother would whip my butt because I'd always be giving someone the bird. Did you guys ever watch them play the guitar?"

Dominic laughed, "That's not what they do. Besides, it's not their middle finger."

Ronnie and Dominic didn't know what they wanted to do. What does it matter when you're 10 or 12? Jimmy had bigger ideas and said, "Everybody knows every kid wants to be a fireman or policeman or a Yankee."

"They do not, you weenie," Dominic said, and when he said "weenie," the conversation quickly died.

Ronnie picked up a *Life* magazine to break the tension, and they scrambled down to the living room floor and crowded around it, head to head. Ronnie was in charge and turned pages until he flipped over the back cover, and there was Jimmy's Yankee hero in a full-page cigarette advertisement. Vic Raschi was looking out from the page with a big smile and a cigarette dangling from his mouth.

The advertisement had a testimony from Raschi, and he was saying, "Camels are my choice for mildness, every time. And Camel's rich, full flavor never tires my taste."

Dominic said, "He smokes cigarettes? How come he's so good?"

Ronnie answered, "Maybe that's what it takes to be a big leaguer."

At once, Ronnie had a marvelous idea. "You guys," Ronnie said, "let's play like we're big leaguers and smoke some cigarettes."

"All right," Dominic exclaimed. "We can play like we're big shots."

Well, if it was good enough for Ronnie and Dominic, then count Jimmy in.

"My parents have some extra packs," Ronnie said.

"Don't you think," Dominic said, "they'll know some will be missing?"

"Ah, they never pay attention," Ronnie said. "They're always at work or go straight to a bar after they get off work."

Jimmy thought, "Heck, it's his house and his neck," and, besides, he had never smoked a cigarette before. "Well, let's do it!" he said out loud, almost cheerfully.

Wherever Ronnie found the cigarettes, he also came out with some matches.

"Well," Jimmy said, "how do you do it?"

"Smoke?" Dominic said. "It's easy. You just take a drag and swallow the smoke." It sounded as if he didn't know how to do it either. But he said the word "drag," and that made it solid information.

"Well," Duane asked, "where does the smoke go? In your stomach?"

Ronnie said, "No, dummy, you just blow it out through your nose."

So, they puffed and puffed, for maybe an hour, nobody knew how to inhale, and the entire pack was gone. The house was full of smoke, and the family Afghan hound knew better because he put his tail between his legs and raced into the back bedroom so he could breathe.

They met again the next day, but had to figure out how to get more cigarettes.

Dominic, who was older and whom Jimmy's father never trusted, had an idea. "Let's write a note from Ronnie's mother and take it to the grocery store at Main Street and Alameda. The old guy who works there will never suspect anything."

"Yeah, good idea," Ronnie agreed and asked: "Who's going to write the note?"

Everybody looked at Jimmy. Ronnie said, "You have the best handwriting. I've seen it. So we pick you."

Jimmy didn't know how he got picked. His handwriting was good, but it wasn't THAT good. Besides, it didn't look like any adult's handwriting that he knew, and certainly not Ronnie's mother's.

Nonetheless, Jimmy became the "writer" of the note and the "mother" who was sending her goody-two-shoes little boy to the grocery store for a pack of cigarettes. They found a pencil, handed it to Jimmy and told him to begin writing.

"I don't know what to say," Jimmy said. "So somebody tell me."

"OK," Ronnie said, "here's what you write: 'I am ill today and can't leave the house. So I am sending my son with 20 cents so he can buy me a pack of cigarettes. Thank you, Edith.' "

Meanwhile, Jimmy still wasn't so sure that he had the best handwriting. He made his letters with big loopy swirls. Jimmy wrote the best he could, but it was still the handwriting of a 10-year-old.

The next question was: Who is going to go into the store? Immediately, they looked at Duane.

"Hey, wait a minute," Duane cried. "Why do I have to be the one to go into the store?"

" 'Cause you're the only one with the guts to do it," Dominic said. "Besides, you jump out of trees. Compared to that, this is a cinch. And your brothers will like you better."

"They will?" Duane said hopefully.

"Sure," Ronnie said. "And you can brag to them. I'll bet they've never done anything like this."

"Well," Duane said, "but only if you think so."

"Of course we think so," Ronnie said, "because we would tell you if we didn't think so."

"I still don't know about this," Duane pleaded. "Why me?"

"Duane," Ronnie said, "the old grocer will never suspect you. Besides, haven't your brothers sent you there before?"

"Well, yeah," Duane said, "but only for an airplane helmet. And Edith is not my mother."

"It doesn't matter," Ronnie said.

"Well, what if he wants to call her on the phone and check?" Duane reasoned.

Dominic had all the answers and said, "Just say she's too sick to talk on the phone."

"OK," Duane said, "but you guys have to go with me."

"We can't all go in the store," Ronnie said. "The grocer will get wise."

"OK," Duane said, "but you can wait outside."

So, off they went on their bicycles, except Dominic. The grocer never had a clue that anything was up. Or maybe he just didn't care. After all, it was a 20-cent sale. Worse, maybe he bought the entire act—handwriting and all. The purchase went off without a hitch, and the boys raced back to Ronnie's house, where Dominic was waiting, and had another smoking party, filling the house again with smoke blown through their noses.

Even with all the butts they created, they were getting smarter and saved enough cigarettes for the next day, which was Friday. But that was all they had, and soon those ran out. Ronnie's parents would be home all weekend, and the boys' tobacco habit would have to wait until Monday.

"We have to plan ahead," Dominic wisely advised. "We have to find a new supply. I don't think we can pull it off again with the old grocer. And Ronnie's parents might get wise." For sure, Ronnie's parents weren't as oblivious as the boys thought.

By now, a nefarious idea was filling Jimmy's head. "I think I know the answer," he said. "I never told you guys, but my grandfather smokes, and he keeps a carton of Wings on the bottom shelf of his bookcase."

"Wings?" Dominic prodded. "Whoever heard of Wings cigarettes?"

"They're real," Jimmy said. "I've seen them."

"OK, OK, how are you going to swipe them?" Ronnie asked.

"Easy," Jimmy said. "He's blind."

Everybody broke into side-splitting laughter. "You're kidding," Ronnie said once he regained control.

"I am not kidding," Jimmy said. "And everybody trusts me and won't suspect a thing. My dad and I go to my grandparents' house every Sunday afternoon for lunch. It'll be a cinch to grab a pack."

"Well," Dominic said, "I don't know how you're going to get them home, but don't smash them in your pants pocket. There's nothing worse than a cig broken in half." By then, Dominic had enough experience to really know about cigs. It was their secret code word for cigarettes.

Jimmy pulled it off without a hint of suspicion, but he fidgeted guiltily in the front seat of his dad's Ford, all the way home from his grandparents' house.

On Monday, only Dominic showed up for the next Yankee-Red Sox battle. He and Jimmy played only for an hour, never referring to Sunday's box score. They were too eager for another smoking party.

"Jimmy, let's go to my house today instead," Dominic said. His divorced mother also worked. "Nobody will be home. And we can glue together some model airplanes, and smoke your Wings the whole time. Get it? Planes and Wings?!"

Dominic laughed at his own cleverness and added, "The smell of smoke won't be a problem because my big brother smokes."

"OK," Jimmy said, "let's go."

Dominic's house was tiny with only one bedroom, a small living room and a kitchen. It was more like a cabin. They opened the model airplane kits, and set a bottle of glue and some airplane dope on the kitchen counter, such as it was. Before they started sanding and gluing and painting, they each lit up a cigarette, puffing away like dashing pilots they'd seen in stirring war movies at El Campo Theater.

Their reverie was broken by scary knocks on the door—rap, rap, rap.

"Who is it?" Jimmy said to Dominic in a panicky whisper.

Dominic peeked out the window over the kitchen sink. "Oh, oh, it's Mrs. Lance!"

Jimmy whined, "She's my Sunday school teacher. What are we gonna do? Please, do something. Please."

"Quick, hide the cigarettes." Now Dominic was in full panic, dragging Jimmy with him. They grabbed pages from a newspaper and began flailing the air.

Mrs. Lance knocked again. It was a deathly sound.

"Good," Dominic said 30 seconds later, "all the smoke is gone. She'll never know. I'm opening the door."

"Are you boys smoking?" she said, knowing full well the answer. She could smell the smoke; she could see the smoke.

Their party went down in smoke. Embarrassed nearly to death, they never said a word as they stuffed the model airplane parts back into their boxes. Jimmy trudged with his head down through deep sand in the vineyard on the path home. The ditch behind his house was in, but he didn't feel like swimming or even playing baseball. Jimmy flopped down in his dad's easy chair and picked up the *Life* magazine. Ronnie had let Jimmy take it home, if he made sure he would bring it back. The curiosity was too much for Jimmy. He was almost compelled to turn the magazine over and look, just one more time, at the back cover with the cigarette ad and his Yankee hero. The bad taste in Jimmy's mouth was still there, though he hadn't given up on his hero, only on smoking, and the worst was yet to come.

On the next weekend, he crawled into the twin bed next to his father's in the quiet of a lazy Saturday morning. The bed had been his mother's, but not since she left. It was peaceful there, if only for a moment more. Jimmy heard his dad's booming voice from only three feet away, as if his words were reverberating across the Grand Canyon:

"Hear you been smoking."

Jimmy froze. "Uh, ah, well," he sputtered and started crying.

"Don't do it again."

Truly, his smoking days were over, and how would he ever be strong enough to play for the Yankees if he smoked? It was still Jimmy's dream.

★ ★ ★

The Yankees continued to pile up victories, on into September, and Jimmy, Ronnie, Dominic and Duane were back in school, as the big league season was winding down. By then, classes took precedence over the games at the Original Edison Field, decades before another one appeared in Anaheim. Their season was over.

It turned out, after all, that the Yankees didn't need Jimmy to help them.

Once again, the Red Sox were the visitors at Yankee Stadium for a five-game series that would wrap up the 1951 season. In the first game, left-handed junk-baller Eddie Lopat shut out the Red Sox. The next day, September 28, hard-throwing right-hander Allie Reynolds added mastery to misery in the first game of a double-header.

The Yankees needed only one win to clinch at least a tie for another American League pennant, their third straight. Reynolds was at his best, if he could pitch any better than he had on July 12 against Cleveland, his former team. He had allowed the Indians no hits.

Against the Red Sox, he had struck out nine and was one out away from victory, leading, 8-0. One newspaper reported,

"Not one Boston batter seemed close to getting a hit." Still, one more dangerous Red Sox batter stood between Reynolds and another no-hitter. Who could be more dangerous than the great Ted Williams?

Reynolds got ahead in the count, and then Williams took a mighty swing. It was a foul pop-up to the right of home plate, not even close to the stands. Catcher Yogi Berra had a clear look at the ball and—dropped it!

Imagine how Berra must have felt—not to mention giving Williams another opportunity! It was simply unthinkable. But Reynolds had the situation under control, telling Berra, "Don't worry, Yogi. We'll get him." Though Williams was not going to hit an eight-run home run, he probably was relishing the idea of breaking up the no-hitter with the second chance.

Reynolds reared back and fired—again Williams took a big cut. It was another high pop-up right in front of home plate. This time, Berra squeezed the ball, and the win and Reynolds' second no-hitter were in the books.

It was the last chance for the Red Sox. It was humiliation at its worst, and, after Reynolds' no-hitter, the Red Sox's desire had leaked completely. Dom DiMaggio, Johnny Pesky, Billy Goodman and Lou Boudreau sat out the rest of the season. What was the use? The Red Sox finished the season in third place, 11 games behind the Yankees.

Always talking baseball, Jimmy and Dominic got into a debate that wouldn't be settled any time soon.

"You know the Yankees have a new centerfielder," Jimmy said, bragging about Mickey Mantle. "He hit a home run in his first game."

Dominic sarcastically came back with: "Yeah, so what? The Giants also have a new centerfielder, Willie Mays."

"Oh, sure, and he didn't get a hit the first 12 times he swung a bat," Jimmy countered.

"Then what happened?" Dominic retorted. "He hit a home run off the best left-handed pitcher in the game, Warren Spahn. And what has Mantle done lately? They shipped him out because he struck out 54 times before June."

"No, he didn't," Jimmy said. "It was 52 times."

"Oh, yeah? 54, 52? So what? It was a lot."

Jimmy knew he was had, so he side-slipped the conversation: "OK, tell me who else is going to be in the World Series." He didn't have to remind Dominic that the Yankees already locked up the American League pennant against his beloved Red Sox.

✶ ✶ ✶

In the other league, the Giants were about to begin a playoff series against the Dodgers. The teams had tied at the end of the regular season, and a best-of-three playoff was scheduled.

When it was still the middle of August, the Dodgers were running away and hiding from the rest of the National League. The Giants were in second place and had good players, but nobody like the Dodger players. It was mediocre vs. the top of the heap. The Dodgers had savvy veterans who knew how to win. They were in the World Series two years before, in 1949, and the Giants hadn't played in the Fall Classic in 14 years.

The Dodgers built a 13½-game lead with a victory in the first game of a double-header on August 12. Meanwhile, the Giants started winning, winning, winning, including a 16-game streak that started on that day.

Jimmy sat in the front seat of the 1948 Ford, listening to the Giants' game and running down the car battery while his dad went into an auto supply store for some inconsequential part. Jimmy didn't think that his dad would have to go back in and ask the store clerk to recharge the Ford's battery.

Instinctively, Jimmy knew there was something going on with the Giants. They were getting hot. The Dodgers knew it, too, and were fatally distracted by watching the scoreboard, and their lead began to crumble. Though Brooklyn didn't play badly, some Dodgers did slump at the plate. On the mound, Ralph Branca's season shifted into reverse gear going from smooth (10 wins, 3 losses) to grinding (3 wins, 10 losses). New York simply caught fire with stingy pitching of low earned-run averages and consistent batting, led by Bobby Thomson's surge of power.

In the first playoff game, Thomson homered off Branca, and the Giants won for a one-game advantage. It was a harbinger of things to come. In the second playoff game, the Dodgers took no prisoners, winning, 10-0. In the final game, they looked as if they would cruise into the World Series against the Yankees, taking a 4-1 lead into the bottom of the ninth.

Then came the fateful rematch of Branca and Thomson at the Polo Grounds, and the most famous home run in all of baseball lore. The Giants scored once and still had two runners on, with Thomson coming to the plate. Waiting on deck was rookie Willie Mays with all of his raw power and youthful zeal. He wouldn't be needed in the ensuing drama, for Thomson hit a hair-raising, three-run home run over the left field wall for a 5-4 win. It was forever more called "The Shot Heard 'Round the World," and the game was further immortalized by Russ Hodges' delirious home-run call: "The Giants win the pennant, the Giants win the pennant, the Giants win the pennant, the Giants win the pennant." The Giants made certain there would be no Dodgers dancing on their hallowed Polo Grounds. It was October 3.

In the World Series, the Giants were no match for the Yankees, losing 4 games to 1.

The next year, the Yankees and Dodgers were back in the Series, and the Yankees prevailed, just as they would over the Dodgers the year after that, in 1953, for their fifth straight World Series title.

Edison Field was getting too small for Jimmy, Ronnie, Dominic and Duane. Jimmy was reunited with his mother and spent the summer of 1953 living with her in Oakville, where he pitched for the town's Little League version of the New York Giants. He struggled at batting, and it was the first time he heard that batting eighth in the lineup is the equivalent of being the second clean-up batter. His coach, Lou Sweet, told him that, and Lou knew baseball.

Lou was a very tall, gangly black man and hit long home runs for the local semipro team. While his young players obviously knew the difference between black and white, they didn't care. Besides, Lou told them he was Hawaiian. That was good enough for them. Who had ever been to Hawaii, anyway? It wasn't good enough for the town, however. Lou coached there only that one summer. There were ugly rumors about him and his wife. But when you're 12 years old, what do you know and what would you care if you did know? Lou would always be the coach who cared enough to take Jimmy and three teammates to watch the Sacramento Solons of the old Pacific Coast League. It was a special time in Lou's bright red Plymouth convertible with the top down, speeding along the two-lane country road. When Jimmy's hat blew off, Lou gladly stopped, turned the car around and searched up and down the road for it. Then, someone thought to look in the back seat and there the hat was all along. Lou didn't mind and laughed along with them.

At one practice session it was Lou who threw the first real curve ball that Jimmy had ever seen. Though Jimmy swore it broke a mile, he did hit it. Even so, the downward force of it almost knocked the bat out of his hands.

It became a magical summer for many other reasons, two foremost in Jimmy's mind: He helped to lead the Giants to the town championship, pitching a no-hitter in the final game of their "World Series"; and his mother never missed one of his games, though he knew full well she had ample opportunities to accept the invitations of single men, for she was still an attractive woman. She was all of 33 years of age.

With the summer over, Jimmy returned to his dad's house in Marshfield. Ronnie never played much baseball again and took up tennis when he was an adult, using his quickness to become a highly rated amateur player. Dominic, his mother and brother moved to another town. Once Jimmy thought he saw Dominic from a distance, but neither of them said anything. Duane's family moved out of state. Years later, Jimmy heard that Duane learned to speak Russian and fly a U-2 spy plane.

One blustery winter's day in 1954, Jimmy and his father were at home alone, and Norman's mother, Evelyn, knocked on their dilapidated screen door. The screen still had pockmarks the size of a 10-inch baseball. When Jimmy opened the front door, Evelyn was standing there holding two baseball mitts.

"Jimmy," she said, quietly, using his name for one of the few times, "Norman is dead. I have these two mitts of his. Why don't you choose one of them?"

She was so near to tears that she couldn't tell the story right then, and probably wouldn't have anyway. No doubt it became the family secret. It was much later when Jimmy's father gave him the rest of the news how Norman and his uncle died. He said, "They were asphyxiated in their one-bedroom apartment. They were drunk, and somehow the gas stove's handle was turned on without any flame." Norman was 19, too young to drink and too young to die.

Jimmy's head was swimming with the sad news, and how could he make a decision about a baseball mitt at a time like this? He looked over the first baseman's mitt, which was a fine specimen with luxurious, thick wool under the wrist strap. But it would take some getting used to, with its strange trapper shape. The catcher's mitt was big and round and looked like a small ottoman. The pocket was big enough only for one baseball. Jimmy looked closer and saw it was a Rawlings Mickey Livingston model, whoever he was. Jimmy had to choose quickly before Evelyn changed her mind and went home. He chose the catcher's mitt. It was a wise choice because all Jimmy wanted to do was pitch for the New York Yankees, and he would always have a catcher's mitt when he needed a friend to catch his pitches. He vowed to keep Norman's catcher's mitt forever.

Sometime around the age of 18, Jimmy gave more thought to a real career, other than playing for the Yankees. He was big enough, at 6 feet, though his weight hadn't caught up with his height, and he eventually got up to 170 pounds. His high school coach, Burley Patterson, told the pitchers to do pull-ups every day. It was mandatory. He said the exercise strengthens the muscles in the upper back—the deltoid, the rhomboid, the teres minor and major, the latissimus dorsi—not forgetting a major tendon under the arm.

Jimmy wasn't a jock major, but took his coach's word that all those muscles are necessary to throw a baseball with "pop." He eventually threw hard enough for some scouts to look at him as he continued at a nearby junior college, but he forgot one thing: the pull-ups. It was a telling flaw for him. Heck, he thought, he was strong enough now, and coaches always were warning that becoming muscle-bound was bad for baseball players.

His coach at the junior college, Frank Myers, demanded that every player be in top shape to contend with all the double-headers on the schedule. Doing 60-yard windsprints daily was mandatory. "Do at least 20 a day," he ordered.

The conditioning regimen and college baseball helped to keep Jimmy's dreams of a professional career alive. Certainly every once in a while someone asked, "Are you being realistic? You'd better have something to fall back on." His father had the same thoughts because a dire pronouncement came from him. He knew little about professional athletes but declared, "You'll never be big enough." That only seemed to prod Jimmy on.

He was, however, thinking about another career and took an interest in sportswriting. He had heard only some things about it, but it looked exciting and glamorous. He could see working for a newspaper, with those huge, loud rotary presses, Linotype machines and hot lead pots, and covering sporting events. Plus, he knew sportswriters got in free to all the games. What could be better than that? Still, that idea also met a brick wall at home. "Where will you ever get a job writing?" his father said. "How will you ever make enough money?"

His father was a product of the Depression, and the specter of eating pork 'n' beans out of a tin can in a hobo's camp must have haunted him, though his family always had enough food on the table. When Jimmy was ready to leave for university, he heard more stifling words from his father: "When you flunk out, you can always come back home." In his clumsy way, his father was trying to assure Jimmy he always had a place to live.

College and romance don't have to go hand in hand, though isn't that the way it often happens? After all, it's that time in life. People are young and free and eager to go their own way, and there's no stopping them. Jimmy was no different. Distracted, he did something else he never imagined he'd do: He forgot about God and church. It was so easy and it almost came naturally, without even thinking about it. Indeed, he wasn't thinking, and it was another moment when he mindlessly forgot the building blocks of his early success.

Predictably, he met a girl just before baseball season began, just when he least expected it or wanted it or needed it, for his dream of playing professional baseball still lived. With seemingly little to say about it, he fell hard for Sally Summers. She was his first love. After baseball, that is. Her beach-blond hair, her inviting smile and her bold Topaze perfume intoxicated him. That's how immature their relationship was. It was fraught with failure. Though they were headstrong and determined to marry, they really didn't know how to make a marriage work.

She showed up for only one of his games, only because a thoughtful roommate at Jimmy's boarding house took her to the stadium for a Saturday afternoon game. Jimmy soon realized that baseball held little interest for her. He ignored the warning signs and thought her belittling remarks about the game were witty, at least for a while. She had doubts about batting helmets. "I thought," she remarked, "that only football players wore helmets." She questioned, as most people do, why players spit so much. "And then they spit on their hands and in their gloves," she said. "And they might even spit on their hands and then pick up dirt and rub them together." Baseball vernacular was something else she couldn't fathom. "What's a twin killing? Do they murder babies?"

Other idiosyncrasies also made no sense to her. "Why do they wear their pants pulled up like Little Lord Fauntleroy?" And: "There he goes again, grabbing his crotch." She was appalled when the opposing bench would mock a player who had just taken a hard ground ball off his shin. "Don't rub it, Meat," they shouted, or worse: "Rub some dirt on it, Meat," knowing, either way, the shin burger was throbbing and burning like fire. Of course, the term "meat" piqued her interest, and the players all seemed to be so manly, except when they would pat each other on their behinds. "And what do they mean," she wondered, "when they say, 'Unbutton your shirt and take a good rip'?"

Looking at players, or scoping them in the players' lingo, did interest her. "All of them are so studly," she said sweetly. As their relationship continued, she became increasingly annoyed at the amount of time Jimmy spent at practice, two or three hours every day after class. And the road trips, though not more than a day or two at a time, ate into her time with Jimmy. After this game, she stayed home and said she had better things to do.

It was Jimmy's first start on the mound for a four-year college, after he transferred from the junior college. He was accustomed to starting the opening game of every double-header, but at the university, there was no pitching rotation or designated pitcher, and he had no idea who would be starting. For that reason or laziness or immaturity, he hadn't arranged for a ride to the stadium from his boarding house clear across town and miles away. Fearing that he would be late for batting practice, Jimmy half-ran, half-walked the entire distance to the stadium. His junior college coach, Frank Myers, would have locked him out of the stadium if he or any other player arrived late. Before one game, Myers ordered the team bus to drive away when that day's starting pitcher was getting out of his car. He had pulled up 30 seconds late. At the university, Jimmy became one of the aces of the staff, but he forgot another basic: the daily windsprints.

On this day, fearing the worst, Jimmy tried to go unnoticed when he tip-toed into the field house and quickly dressed in the white home uniform. Of course, he couldn't hide the click-clack-click of his spikes on the concrete floor as he left. Once outside, Jimmy sprinted to the stadium and half-sneaked in. Breathing easier, now that he had made it safely, he avoided the dugout where his college coach, Fred Williams, was making out the lineup card. Jimmy hoped he could hide among other players in the bullpen. But here came Williams, striding purposefully toward Jimmy. He thought he was had.

"Here," Williams said, "you're the starting pitcher today." He tossed a white, shiny baseball to him.

Jimmy was relieved, or was he? The opponent was one of the best teams in the nation. He had heard about their fearsome lineup of batters who swung with both feet coming off the ground. There were 20 minutes until game time, and that fit easily into his warm-up routine. He needed only 15 minutes to warm up, and his routine wasn't very elaborate. He threw a few easy pitches midway between the catcher and the mound, and then climbed the hill. As he threw harder and harder and neared the end of the 15 minutes, the starting shortstop came over.

"You ready?" he said. Though a three-year veteran, he had strangely little knowledge about a pitcher's routine of putting on his game face.

Surly, Jimmy grunted, "How should I know?"

He quickly found out in the top of the first inning. The leadoff batter singled. The second batter grounded sharply to the veteran shortstop. It was a perfect double-play ball. But the shortstop fumbled the ball and was lucky to get a force out. The next batter also grounded sharply to the veteran shortstop. It was a repeat, another bobble, but at least another force out. The inning should have been over. Fortunately, Jimmy struck out the cleanup batter, and no runs scored. Meanwhile, his team couldn't solve the opposing pitcher.

The score stayed 0-0 for five innings, despite one unnerving moment. Jimmy saw his friend and sweetheart walk into the stadium, and he threw a rainbow of a pitch that missed the batter, the catcher, the umpire and almost the backstop. Laughs and hooting were heard from the opposing dugout, and everyone on Jimmy's team believed the sight of her caused him to lose control. Unlikely to convince them later that he was trying to throw a changeup that got away, he let them have their joke.

Then, with two outs in the sixth inning, Jimmy walked the catcher. Up came the burly first baseman. Jimmy quickly threw two strikes. On the next pitch, the first baseman hit a high pop-up halfway between home plate and first base, and about 10 feet into foul ground. The catcher had no idea where the ball was, and it fell untouched. Jimmy knew he could have caught it himself, but he was told somewhere along the way, "Let your fielders do their job." He forgot the other half of the corollary: "Once the pitcher lets the ball go, he becomes the ninth fielder." With the count still 0 and 2, Jimmy planned to buzz him with a high hard one and then fool him with a sweeping curve ball away. Instead, the intended brush-back pitch wasn't in far enough, and the batter hammered a two-run home run.

That was the way the game ended, and it was a harbinger of the run support he got the entire season. His team had had the bases loaded three times and couldn't score. The coach was always teaching about hitting the bottom half of the baseball, and they were just trying to hit any part of it, and didn't.

On other days, Jimmy simply didn't have it. "Too many bases on balls," Williams growled, stomping around in the dugout. "You're trying to be too fine." And Jimmy was. But it seemed he was better pitching behind in the count, and with runners on base. It may have been because he hid the ball better in the stretch than out of a full windup. Either way, he loved to pitch from behind and in the stretch.

Once, Jimmy walked the leadoff batter. Then, he walked the second batter. Williams was somewhat mollified as Jimmy picked the runner off second base. They had practiced a pickoff play that nobody on his team had used until that moment. The runner on first base must not have been watching Jimmy's quickness and took a large lead. Without throwing another pitch to the plate, Jimmy pivoted and caught the eager runner leaning. Two outs, just like that. The coach tried to feign indifference, as many coaches do, not wanting to let a player get the big head. But the coach couldn't hide his elation. "Atta boy," he yelled.

One March night, Jimmy was getting hit hard, and he refused to pay attention to the bullpen. He always finished what he started. Sure, he had thrown eight innings, and, all right, they were hitting him hard, but he was getting outs. Still, Williams knew what he was doing and wanted to protect a win for Jimmy.

Not every player on the team agreed with Williams, who relied more on textbook theory than on baseball instinct, and one of the rebels was Mike Long, also a pitcher. In a team meeting before a game, Mike interrupted the coach as he went over the lineup and asked him point-blank: "There is no pitching rotation, so how do you decide who will pitch? Do you use a Ouija board, or what?" Mike was the same player who stole baseballs by burying them in the dirt in the bullpen and sneaking back into the stadium at night to retrieve them. And when Williams started wearing a toupee, Mike didn't recognize him standing in the center of a group of other coaches and blurted out in front of everybody: "Anybody seen Heady Freddy?" Mike lived to pitch another day. In fact, he was the team's winningest pitcher. He got plenty of run support.

Fred Williams yanked Jimmy that night, and the next day they were playing an away game in the San Francisco Bay Area. That university's program was so big it had a trainer, assistant trainers and a training room. Having thrown those eight innings the night before, Jimmy was sitting in the bullpen and thought it was safe to disappear midway in the game. Mike—it was always Mike who was up to no good—convinced him. "Hey, you pitched last night," he said. "Let's go." They walked over to the university's gymnasium and up the stairs to the training room. "What do you boys need?" the trainer asked. He was more than pleased to help them. After each received an arm massage, they returned to the bullpen unnoticed.

No sooner had Jimmy sat back down, with his uniform in disarray and his shirttail hanging out than Heady Freddy yelled, "Get warm. You're going in." It was the bottom of the ninth, runners at the corners, the tying and winning runs, if they scored. In a matter of several seconds and only a few throws, Jimmy was in the game facing a batter who was already a star quarterback and an All-American. Jimmy threw him a sharp hook for strike one. That's 12 to 6 on your kitchen clock. The second pitch was a sweeping curve. The quarterback hit enough of it for a two-hopper to the shortstop for a force out, ending the game and preserving the victory.

It was one of several high points in his up-and-down season. Odds were that the next game against a Central Coast opponent wouldn't go as well. There was nothing special about the team; it wasn't a baseball power. At the same time, there was everything special about it. A few players had been on the school's football team two years earlier. On a return flight from a game in the Midwest, the charter plane crashed on takeoff, and 16 were killed. The school was devastated, and the nation was shocked. Within a short time, the Mercy Bowl football game was organized as a fund-raiser for the families and players. Some made heroic recoveries after horrible injuries and the trauma of losing many teammates. That day, Jimmy was out-pitched by one of the injured survivors.

The game after that also didn't go so well. In the thin air of Reno, a curve ball doesn't bite as much, and a batted ball carries and carries. It was another loss.

With the coming of Easter vacation, the team traveled to a tournament with the top teams in Southern California. The opening game was scheduled against a team that was ranked No. 4 in the nation. Before the game, Jimmy was horsing around with his teammates down the right-field line when here came Heady Freddy with another shiny baseball: "Fletcher, you're starting this game, and I'm not asking you to win. I'm telling you to win." It was the kick in the pants he needed. He pitched a complete-game victory, though he needed a home run from his first baseman in the bottom of the ninth to break a tie for the win. On two days' rest, he faced the 15th-ranked team and shut them down, losing a shutout only because of an error. Though there would be other victories, there was no disputing that this week was the highlight of his season.

Home from college, Jimmy caught on with two semipro teams. One night, he pitched seven strong innings against a semipro team loaded with university players and several ex-pros. The next night, for the other team, he was needed and came in relief. On the third straight night, he was in the bullpen and told to warm up. He tried, but he just couldn't go, feeling weakness—not the usual soreness—in his arm. One of the teams folded, and the other team stopped calling him.

By the summer of 1962, Jimmy's allegiance to the Yankees was starting to wane, mainly because of the proximity of a National League team, the San Francisco Giants. Major league baseball had come to the West Coast four years earlier with the arrival of the Dodgers and Giants. Not only did he consider the Dodgers "the enemy," but also he simply liked the Giants, and there was that Little League season when he played for "the N.Y. Giants."

With the fall came the World Series Jimmy always hoped would never happen. The Yankees were still his team, certainly as far as the American League was concerned, but he often asked himself: "What if my Yankees and the Giants ever meet in the World Series? Who will I root for?" He truly was torn, even before Willie McCovey hit that screaming line drive that Yankee second baseman Bobby Richardson caught, reaching above his head without jumping, for the final out in the seventh game, with the potential tying run on third base and Willie Mays on second. McCovey's at-bat went down as one of the most famous in the history of the game—alongside Bobby Thomson's home run and Babe Ruth's "call shot" home run in the 1932 World Series against the Chicago Cubs. Deep inside, Jimmy was happy the Yankees won.

Before the start of the next college season, Mike Long, ever the wise guy, was serious for a change and asked Jimmy to join him for a workout in the university's gym. They threw a little, and then started to run some windsprints on the hardwood floor on the upper level. The windows were open, although it was January. Some rain had come in, and, unknown to them, there were small, invisible puddles on the floor. As Jimmy started to slow down, his heel hit a puddle and he skidded hard on his tailbone. After the initial pain eased, Jimmy and Mike thought nothing of the incident. But the first time Jimmy tried to throw batting practice, there was no strength in his arm. He could throw as hard as he wanted, certainly, but the ball had no movement. He suddenly had a very effective changeup if only for one or two pitches. After that, he was hit hard, and he had no command of his pitches. Throwing a ball down the center of the plate was becoming more and more difficult. His right shoulder became increasingly weak, and his coach knew that a shoulder injury was terminal for a prospective pitcher. Jimmy threw only 15 innings that season, down from 90 one year earlier. As it turned out, his career had peaked in that 1962 season.

Jimmy never made it to the Yankees.

It was the second tragedy in his young life—after his parents' divorce. Two more were on the other side of the horizon.

His baseball prospects over, his sweetheart was convinced he would spend all of his time with her, and never more waste time with baseball. They did marry and had one daughter, born in 1964. Jimmy finished college with a degree in journalism and caught on at the small daily newspaper in Oakville, where his mother still lived.

As a struggling journalist at a small paper, he was making only $55 a week, and their marriage struggled also.

"Is that it?" she said, looking at his reporter's meager paycheck. "Is this what you went to college for? That's pitiful."

She was unhappy from the start, and infidelity was building a head of steam and only a whistle stop away. She thought, "I knew this would never work, so why did I marry this loser in the first place?" She conveniently forgot that they had a beautiful daughter.

While Jimmy was in the press box nightly at the ball park or every Friday night in the fall at the high school football stadium, his wife caught the eye of a local coach who had been scoping the crowd, and it was all their fragile marriage didn't need. Their marriage survived for the usual two reasons: Jimmy knew nothing about the affair, and the coach wouldn't divorce his wife. He had young children, in addition to major financial investments he couldn't risk losing, so divorce was out of the question. The affair lasted for five years, longer than Jimmy's marriage. And Jimmy's wife? She had the best of all worlds—a nice home and a lover on the side—and she was bullet-proof, thinking she would never be discovered. When Jimmy finally woke up, he was distraught over his stupidity. He thought, "How could I have been so blind and the last to find out?" Especially in a town of only 9,000 people, where everybody knew whose car was parked in his driveway, while he was covering out-of-town games? This thought went through his mind more often than she called him pathetic: "Is nothing sacred enough to withstand the oncoming locomotive of infidelity?"

Ever the romantic, Jimmy tried to save the marriage, not even knowing why or how it possibly could be saved. When his wife refused to give up her boyfriend, Jimmy had no recourse but divorce. His wife got almost everything she wanted—freedom, their daughter—but not the boyfriend. She later married someone else and was the bitter one. There was no money to divide, so their daughter became her pawn, and she expressed her bitterness by telling him, "You'll never see her again, if I have anything to say about it." Jimmy's hands were tied. It was 1968.

In one fell swoop, divorce had hit him again, and he lost his daughter, who had become the treasure of his life.

Oakville was near the state capital, Sacramento, which had had a Triple A baseball team since the 1920s. Though Jimmy was not yet truly a journeyman writer, he was given his first big assignment to cover the team, probably as much for his knowledge of the game as for his writing ability. He did grow into the job, learning the game at a deeper level from players on their way up to the big leagues and on their way down, and from grizzled managers who had been in the game since the 1940s. The beat was his for the next 20 years, and he made the cramped, hot, wooden press box his sanctuary. After his wife moved to another state, he poured his energy into the game and the craft he loved. He always harbored this thought: "Maybe, just maybe, she'll relent and I'll see my daughter on school vacations, just like I saw my mother." She never did. His daughter, Jennifer, had just turned 4, and he never saw her again until one special day in 1982. He was then 42, and she was 18.

Part Two

Although Jennifer was too young to know the difficulties involved in searching some day for the father she never really knew, she had an inborn sense that she needed to do it. It became her secret quest.

She was barely 4 when she last saw her father, and she blocked out the year along with the pain. Buried along with her pain was any memory of the night Jimmy and Sally fought once, long after Jennifer had gone to bed. Awakened by the shouting, she stumbled, half awake, into their bedroom. For years after, she had recurrent nightmares and walked in her sleep.

So it was that her image of Jimmy Fletcher kept growing fuzzier and fuzzier, almost to the point of fading completely. Who could have kept it alive? Certainly, her mother was the last person to volunteer any information about him. Whenever the topic of conversation about him got a little too close for comfort, her mother told her he was unimportant, not a part of her life, and didn't need to be because she had a stepfather and he was enough. That was all. Still, Jennifer's dream would not be squelched.

Jennifer ultimately figured out it was one of their colossal blunders, and she resented it. She vaguely remembered only their devious reasons. Eventually, her curiosity surfaced and built relentlessly, always nagging at her for answers. But whom could she have asked?

As her teen-age years came, she wondered secretly, "Why don't they be adults and say, 'Jennifer, we think it's time you meet your real father and get to know him'?" She knew her bitter mother would have spit out of her mouth such a ridiculous notion. If there was any one characteristic implicit in her mother's makeup, it was inflexibility. Once she made up her mind, there was no changing it. And the words that dictated how she lived her life were those haunting words to Jimmy: "You'll never see her again, if I have anything to say about it."

This is the way Jennifer looked at it: Not only was it a decision that didn't make any sense, but it was also hers to change. There would be no stopping her.

Still, a more practical question remained: Did Jennifer even have enough details to start off in the right direction? Some information had truly seeped into her memory bank, probably by osmosis, as they say, when a sympathetic friend of her mother's casually let some information slip out from time to time. Jennifer had a pretty good idea of where to look.

Jennifer would be traveling a long way from home, and, while she was accustomed to taking vacation trips with her mother and stepfather, this would be her first time of going alone, out of state, first to Marshfield, where Jimmy grew up (she was certain of that), and then to Oakville, where he lived and worked (at least she thought so).

Her route would take her across two states, great expanses of desert, through a mountain range and several large cities, even though the Interstates effectively skirted them. And a single girl traveling alone? How smart was that? Her car was a matronly 10-year-old sedan that looked like an overturned bathtub. Her parents gave it to her as a graduation present so she could have a car in college. But what if it broke down in one of those deserted places along the Interstate? She had never changed a tire by herself. Sure, her parents had given her instructions and she knew her home telephone number, but weren't those telephone booths sort of creepy and smelly? Someone could be hiding in them, or nearby.

She had to convince them that she would be all right. At first, they knew only she was going to California. They thought, "Maybe Disneyland or up the coast to San Francisco."

"I might even go to the town where I was born," she said when she revealed a little more of her plan and uttered "Oakville." Her dream was out of the bag.

"You're going where?!" her mother shrieked when she told them. "I suppose you're going to look for your father! Well, you will not!"

"Why can't I?" Jennifer said, keeping her argument simple without crossing over to her mother's side of hysteria.

"Because . . . because . . . because," her mother stuttered, "you just can't!"

"I think it's time," Jennifer said, ignoring her mother's lack of logic. "I'm 18 years old."

While her stepfather sat silently by (it was his milk-toast manner), her mother finally gave in to Jennifer's adventuresome spirit, though it took days for her to come around. She must have come to realize that Jennifer's desire to see him was irrepressible and there was nothing she could do about it. The thought of taking away the car never entered her mind.

✱ ✱ ✱

The Interstate highway across the Mojave Desert in California is almost as straight as it is boring. Just as wearing are the 115-degree temperatures. Fortunately, Jennifer's aging car—the upside-down bathtub—had air-conditioning that was very good, and she could stay fresh, sort of. With every uneventful hour after hour, she passed through Blythe and San Bernardino and the northern part of the Los Angeles Basin, and then over the cooler Tehachapi Mountains. She thought the mountain scenery was pretty but not what she would call spectacular. Descending from the Ridge Route into the Central Valley and into Bakersfield, she had to turn on the air-conditioner again.

The Interstate soon takes off in a direction to the west, though it's so subtle that you hardly know it, and she was now on Highway 99, still pushing north to the middle of California. She had been on the road for six hours already, and it would be at least six more hours before she reached Marshfield. She decided it was time to pull off 99 and find a motel in Bakersfield. She figured she would reach Marshfield by the middle of the next day, and what was the hurry? Well, there was some sense of urgency because she shivered nervously each time she thought of that first meeting, especially after years of wondering about her father, this man who was a mystery. While she had caught only bits and pieces about him, none of it sounded very good, or at least that was the tone of those adult conversations she overheard.

Jennifer thought he couldn't be a bad man. After all, her mother married him. Otherwise, she asked herself, why would she be rushing into the world of possibly a criminal or an ex-con or a pedophile? Surely she didn't know what she was getting into. Little did she know he was only a sportswriter.

Ever since she was about 7 or 8 years old, she had an empty feeling in her life, without a real father. Though she knew her stepfather wasn't her father, she called him "Dad" anyway. That fact wasn't hidden from her. But she used "Dad" only in that cloying way that daughters-in-law call their husband's parents "Mom" and "Dad." She always thought that was weird. So where was her real father? Her mother's friend gave only vague hints. "He's a newspaperman or something," she'd say. Or: "He lives in a small town or somewhere." Or: "He lives in Northern California." If nobody had the guts to tell her the details, then she needed to have the guts to find out by herself.

And why was her mother withholding her past from Jennifer? She loved her mother, but Jennifer didn't want her to die and never know the truth. Was there a black chapter in her mother's life that needed to be buried with her generation? Was there a dark secret about her father? She had heard of kids who imagined their dad had been in prison, when he hadn't been, but there always was a period that was unaccounted for and always hush-hush. The dad's driver license photo may even have resembled a jail mug shot. Maybe all kids go through this. Or they think their parents aren't really theirs, especially when everybody in the family has dark hair, and the children are blond. At some age these fears vanish like all childhood fears do, and they later bring smiles when kids look back and think they were so childish. But at the time these thoughts were as real as creepy creatures in the night.

Jennifer arose the next day, had breakfast and found a service station with reasonable prices, surprising because gasoline prices had reached $1.40, and she got back on 99 and headed north. Six uneventful hours later, she drove into Marshfield, which had one traffic light in the middle of town. She found a lunch counter at a corner drug store and began her search for Jimmy by casually engaging the waitress not much older than herself.

"Do you know anybody around here named Jimmy Fletcher?" she started.

Nearly everybody at the counter turned and answered as if on cue: "Of course we know Jimmy."

The volunteers continued their answers.

"Everybody knows him."

"He was born here, grew up here and then went away to college."

"A real good ballplayer."

"Are you looking for him?"

She said, "Well, yes."

"You don't look like you could be the FBI, you're too young, and I haven't seen his picture on the post office wall, so he can't be Wanted." It was a small-town joke.

"No, I'm not the FBI."

"Well, how do you know him?"

"I don't actually know him. I mean, I used to know him, and I hardly know anything about him."

The group's designated spokesman said, "I can tell you he works at the paper up in Oakville. I think it's called the *Oakville Register*."

"I want to find out some things about him before I go up there and meet him. I want to be prepared and know what to expect."

"OK, I'll tell you where you can start. His old baseball coach lives right down the street, across from the high school baseball diamond. His name is Burley Patterson, and his number is 278 N. Poplar."

"That's great. Thanks," she said. She finished her sandwich and drove down the street the high school was on. There was Burley's house on the left with a 1956 Chevrolet pickup parked in the driveway. She was well-versed about baseball to immediately recognize a couple of beat-up Louisville Sluggers lying in the bed of the truck.

"Yeah, Jimmy was a good high school player," Burley recalled. "Nothing special, but good. He got better when he matured physically and got some more games under his belt. Especially in junior college and at the university."

Burley was a man of few words, and he kindly directed her to one of Jimmy's earliest coaches, Mr. Taylor.

"Jimmy had to learn how to hit, and it wasn't easy for him," Mr. Taylor said. "But I'll tell you this much: He could always bunt. He had a soft touch, and he never fouled one off. I could rely on him for a sacrifice bunt. Too bad his arm gave out, and he never played pro ball, or got signed by the Yankees. Of course, this here is Giant territory. None of those Dodger fans around here."

Jennifer next found Jimmy's seventh-grade English teacher who had recruited him to recite a poem at Marshfield's yearly PTA talent show. "He memorized that poem in no time at all," Mrs. Lupin remembered. "It was named *Just Before Christmas* by Eugene Field." Mrs. Lupin's eye lids fluttered and her eyes rolled back into her head, and she started quoting it:

Father calls me William, sister calls me Will,
Mother calls me Willie, but the fellers call me Bill!
Mighty glad I ain't a girl—ruther be a boy,
Without them sashes, curls, an' things that's worn by
    Fauntleroy!
Love to chawnk green apples an' go swimmin' in the
    lake—
Hate to take the castor-ile they give for bellyache!
'Most all the time, the whole year round, there ain't no flies
    on me,
But jest 'fore Christmas I'm as good as I kin be!

"Well, you get the idea," she said, returning to this world, and Jennifer was relieved when Mrs. Lupin came to her senses because there was more, and it went on and on. "On stage, when he recited it, he wore this coonskin hat. It was real, not one of those Davy Crockett Fess Parker fakes. He told me his sister's cat attacked it several times, the wild smell was so strong, and he had a bamboo cane to go with his britches that had a hole in the knee. He looked like a real Huck Finn. He was one of my favorites."

She gave Jennifer the name of his high school journalism teacher, a good-looking but shy Southerner who had stayed in the West after he served in the Navy during the Korean War. Mr. Lewis gave a good account of Jimmy, too.

"He didn't know much about writing or journalism when he started his senior year," Mr. Lewis said. "Not even the five W's, and certainly he wrote his first news story as if it were a melodrama. But I'm not surprised he is working at a newspaper now. He turned into a good writer, and he wrote an obituary that was Class A No. 1 when his very first Little League coach, Mr. Sweet, I believe his name was, died. That was up in Oakville. I also heard Jimmy nearly got in trouble when he dug into Oakville's first murder case in over 25 years. He found out that one of the town's city fathers was mixed up in a triangle love relationship, though nothing came of it. But he has a good nose for news, even in that small town where there are some deep, nasty secrets." It was obvious that Jennifer had the same investigative traits and perseverance, having tracked down all these important people who gave her valuable insight into her father.

When she reached Oakville, she picked up a newsstand copy of the *Oakville Register* and read that the nearby Triple A team was at home that night, across the river in Sacramento. The game was scheduled to begin at 7:15, and she drove into the parking lot in plenty of time to walk through the ballpark and see exactly how to get up to the press box. There was a man in the radio booth, but the open area where the writers sat was empty. Then she saw two men making their way from the field up to the press box. She thought Jimmy might be one of them, though she couldn't tell. If he was one of them, then he certainly didn't fit her image of him, thin and trim. Those two guys were beyond their playing weight, if they, indeed, ever played.

She waited a few minutes and climbed the steps. There was no usher to stop her or ask her for a press pass, and she peeked into the press box. There were the two beat writers from the Sacramento papers.

"Hi," she said tentatively and looked directly at the man she thought might be him, "are you Jimmy Fletcher?"

He turned and answered, "No, Jimmy will be up in a minute. He works out and takes infield practice with the Sacramento team. He's probably changing his clothes."

She was relieved that he most likely was still thin and trim.

One of the writers told her, "Please pull up a chair. He won't be long." However, Jimmy didn't show up until the bottom of the first inning was over, and for good reason.

When Jimmy came through the press box door, she stood to greet him.

"Uh, you don't know me," she said, still hesitant, "but can we talk for a second? Maybe in private?"

"Sure. Just outside the other end of the press box, in the stands."

They were out of earshot of the other two writers, and there weren't enough people in the park to be in that section and bother them.

"I don't know who you are, but what's up?" he said.

"My name is Jennifer. I'm your daughter."

It hit him as if a black hole had sucked all the air out of him. His knees buckled for a moment, and his head spun. He tried to deal with the sentence handed down by the judge and jury—his ex-wife—that he would never see her again if she had anything to do with it.

"Uh, well, uh," he mumbled. "How do you do? I mean, I'm glad to see you. What brings you to Sacramento?" His response was stiff, awkward, as if he was talking to a total stranger, and, of course, he was.

"I'm fine," she said politely, and her softness gave him some time to recover. He noticed immediately that they had an affinity as if they had never been apart.

"Please sit down," he said, "inside the press box."

"Isn't it against the rules for a woman to be in the press box?"

"No, there are no written rules."

"Are you sure?"

"Of course. It's just that there are not many women sportswriters, and it always has been a man's sanctuary at the ball yard."

Jimmy began to loosen up. "There are exceptions, though. Like the Goody Girl."

"The Goody Girl? Who or what is that?"

Jimmy laughed. "She's the girl from the concessions stand who comes up to the press box and takes orders from us writers. Like Cokes or hot dogs or sausage sandwiches. You know, whatever is on the menu. And everything is free. The team pays."

"Oh, hmm, the Goody Girl!"

"So I think we have a precedent, and regardless we can make an exception," he said, smiling. "Please be my guest. Here, let's go meet the other writers. This is Dirk Brown from *The Sacramento*

Bee, and this is Sam Johnson from *The Sacramento Union*. You guys, please meet Jennifer . . . uh . . . ."

She stepped in to ease his awkwardness: "Fletcher."

"Yes, Fletcher. She's my daughter."

The two other writers welcomed her again. "I see the resemblance, but Jimmy, I didn't know you had a daughter," said Brown.

"Well, I wasn't so sure either," Jimmy said. "It was a long time ago."

Jimmy and Jennifer moved to the far end of the press box, first, so they wouldn't disturb the others but, mainly, to have privacy so they could talk. The second inning already had started, and Jimmy laid out his scorebook and pen to his right, and his portable typewriter in front of him. Jennifer sat on his left.

"Now, then, Jennifer," he said, "what does bring you to Sacramento? Surely not to see a baseball game."

"No, I can watch baseball any time. I just graduated from high school and . . ."

"How old are you now?" he broke in, as if he needed to be reminded that she was born in 1964 on January 9.

"18," she said.

"And you're living in . . ."

"Phoenix."

He didn't want to reveal how much he knew, so he said: "Ah, yes, it seems to ring a bell. So . . . how did you know how to find me, and why would you want to?"

"Well, first, people in Marshfield helped me, along with a friend of my mother's."

Jennifer told him some of the story about her journey across the desert and up to Marshfield and then Oakville and over to Sacramento. All of that was true, and she momentarily avoided answering the second half of his question.

"And the other question?" Jimmy said, slightly pressing as any good reporter would.

She fidgeted a little and looked down at the scorebook. "I've always had, what I call, a hole in my heart . . . ."

"You mean something you were born with, a congenital problem?" he said, half-teasing her.

"No, I mean about missing you all the years I was growing up. And I needed you and wanted to find you."

Those were the gaps that could never be filled in. He wasn't there when Jennifer lost her first baby tooth or when she had her first crush on a boy in the first grade. He couldn't watch her dress up in one of his business shirts or teach her to ride a bicycle. He couldn't dry her tears when her first boyfriend broke up with her because he "liked" her best friend better.

"Sorry if I was being a little coy. I think I know about holes in my heart. I've got a few, too, Jennifer."

"Please call me Jenny," she said. "Can I call you Dad?"

"Of course." He would have said more, but the words stuck in the lump in his throat. At the same time, his face beamed with pride. As he smiled, a tear was almost squeezed from his eye, but it really wasn't a tear, not really.

"But, Jenny," he said after the pause, "how did you recognize me?"

"Well, I didn't. I should have known because your features are a little familiar, and you certainly are in better condition than those other writers."

Jimmy laughed modestly. "I try to keep myself in shape. I always said that when I quit playing baseball after college, I would try to stay active. I still play softball, and I learned how to play tennis. I wish I'd have learned tennis when I was little, but my father always said that all tennis players are skinny. I didn't want to be skinny, but, heck, I was anyway. But, now, I can't throw anywhere near how I could in college.

"I apologize for getting up here a little late, after the game started. The reason is, I took ground balls during batting practice. A writer certainly couldn't do that in the big leagues, but here in Triple A, well, they allow it. And after I changed my clothes, I thought I'd watch the Phoenix pitcher from dugout level. You couldn't do that in the big leagues, either. The umpire would run you out of there in a second, and he'd make a big deal of it, and all the fans would know, just because he has to show who's boss. Of course it is a rule that anyone in the dugout has to be in uniform, or at least official."

Jimmy had watched the Phoenix pitcher, John Maglia, allow a leadoff single in the bottom of the first inning. Then, Maglia struck out the next three batters, and, as Jimmy and Jennifer got settled in, he fanned the next three in the bottom of the second. He whiffed the first two in the bottom of the third before a punch-and-judy hitter reached base on a 140-foot bleeder of a hit.

Jennifer was watching closely. "Wow," she said, "eight consecutive strikeouts." She added that he was throwing a really nasty slider. "Maybe," she said, "it could be a slurve."

"Well, it sounds like you know a little about baseball," Jimmy said.

"Thank you. You see, I've been a fan since I was 8 years old. It was the first season that I followed a whole season, and that was the year that the Oakland A's won the pennant and then beat the Cincinnati Reds in seven games in the World Series."

"That's right, and you certainly have a good memory."

"Well, here's something else about that Series," she said, proud about her knowledge of the game. "All of the games, except one, were decided by one run, and not many runs were scored, so there was some outstanding pitching." She rattled off such names as Catfish Hunter, Rollie Fingers, Vida Blue, Jack Billingham, Pedro Borbon. "And especially against all those great hitters." She threw out more names from both rosters: Bando, Tenace, Bench, Morgan, Perez, and the Hall of Fame managers, Dick Williams and Sparky Anderson.

Jimmy smiled and asked: "But no Reggie Jackson?"

"No, he got hurt right at the end of the season and wasn't on the roster."

The talk about the "Swinging A's" and the "Big Red Machine" continued, while some drama was developing with Maglia, the Phoenix pitcher, who was on his way to racking up a total of 13 strikeouts. Despite the strikeouts, the game moved smartly along, and the Sacramento team went out 1-2-3 in the bottom of the ninth.

Jimmy made a quick tour of both clubhouses for a couple of quotes and returned to the press box to start writing his story for the next day's *Oakville Register*. His usual assignment was to write 15 column inches, though he could go over occasionally. With such a stellar pitching performance, he used that extra allowance for three more inches.

In his story, Jimmy wrote, "The eight strikeouts in a row tied a Pacific Coast League record set in September 1910 by Vean Gregg of Portland against the Los Angeles Angels." That was 72 years earlier, almost to the month, because it was the middle of August 1982.

Jimmy finished batting out his story and put his typewriter in its case. He and Jenny walked out of the empty stadium toward the parking lot. They had been so absorbed with the game that Jimmy hadn't bothered to ask her whether she had a place to stay. Of course, she didn't have a hotel room that night.

"OK, I am inviting you to be my guest for as long as you want to stay," Jimmy said. "I have two extra bedrooms. Well, one is my office, and the other is for guests. You can have it."

Jenny wanted to be certain he was serious, so she asked: "You aren't married? Or at least have a girl friend?"

"No," Jimmy said, "it's just me and my house. No dog. No cat. No bird."

✳ ✳ ✳

Jimmy poured a couple of soft drinks for them as they sat at his kitchen table.

"Tell me about yourself," Jimmy said.

"I just graduated from high school, and I plan to go to the state university this fall. I want to major in sports medicine."

"That's a good occupation, and I see a lot more women in that profession."

"But, Dad, what do you do? I mean besides being a sportswriter."

"That's about it, ever since you and your mother left. That's been 14, 15 years. I don't know exactly." Of course he knew exactly, having counted every day and week since.

Mentioning her mother, Jimmy had broached the subject, giving tacit approval to plumb the depths of what happened between them.

"Dad," Jennifer said, "tell me what happened and why you never came to see me."

"Well, Jenny," he started, trying to remember the lines he'd mentally rehearsed if this meeting ever came to pass, "the answer to your first question is, you probably should talk to your mother about it. I mean, I finally realized what went on, but I'm certain she has a different story."

"But, Dad, she would always stop any conversation like that cold. I don't know why she'd be open about it now."

"I see what you mean," Jimmy said. "It sounds like her. Well, about your second question, the answer may be the same. I wanted to come to see you, but your mother, well, she stopped any possibility of that cold, too. I know my answers aren't very good, and they sound like excuses as weak as water, but they're the truth."

"Well, didn't you ever try?"

"I did, and I phoned several times, but she always stopped me, and after a while, she'd just hang up on me. It's something she is good at. So, I quit trying, always hoping she would wake up and know that you need to know your real father. Of course, I needed you, too. So I take responsibility for failure on my part."

"Didn't you try writing? I'm sure you had the address."

"I wrote many letters and sent cards on your birthday, even before you could read. I guess you didn't get them."

"No, I never saw any mail from you."

"So," he said, "I quit trying that, too, when I got no answer. Then, I thought that one day she might bring you here or let you come on your own."

"That's what I did on this trip," Jennifer said. "I made up my mind to do what would never happen otherwise. Well, I have to say that I'm glad I did."

"Yes," Jimmy said, "I am glad, too. It was a real surprise when you introduced yourself. So, let's get some rest, and we can go out to breakfast and get to know each other better over the next few days. The team has 10 more days on this home stand, and you're welcome to stay that long or longer. You can get to know the manager—he's called "Jaws"—and the team's trainer. His name is Harry. I'm sure he can show you some things about being a trainer, but I warn you: He's from the old school."

✳ ✳ ✳

That night, they were back in the press box for another game against Phoenix. This time, it was an outstanding pitching performance by the Sacramento pitcher. Left-hander Gary Bell was tying the Phoenix batters in knots. Bell threw a heavy ball and kept it low the entire game. He finished with a seven-hitter and a 5-0 victory.

Jimmy was the first of the three writers to reach Bell in the Sacramento clubhouse. Of course, he wanted to know the reason for Bell's success in what obviously was a game that turned his season and his career around. Only a week before, the Phoenix team hit Bell so hard that he was ready to demand a trade. His bravado was fueled by the bourbon whiskey he was drinking straight from a bottle at the hotel bar.

"I might need to change uniforms," Bell declared to Jimmy and to anybody else who would listen. By morning, he had thought better of his demands, and Jimmy already had decided not to write about the episode. Later, Bell credited Jimmy with saving his career, and he thanked Jimmy every time the opportunity came up. Jimmy only smiled, knowing he did little.

On this night, Bell was in front of his locker and started to pull off his sweat-heavy wool undershirt.

"First," he said, "I have to give credit for my success tonight to my Lord and Savior, Jesus Christ."

Jimmy stopped him cold. "Cut out that crap and tell me about the game," he said harshly.

It was an early test of Bell's Christian testimony, because he only recently became a Christian. Bell was taken aback for an instant, then ignored Jimmy's remark and said, "I knew I had to win, and the only thing I thought about between starts was keeping the ball down. Even warming up, I was throwing the ball high." His catcher Glenn Hardy told him to follow through, and the tip worked.

Out at the car, Jennifer was waiting. "Did you interview Bell?"

"Sure did," Jimmy said.

"What did he have to say?"

"Oh, he wanted to talk about Jesus."

"And, Dad, what did you say when he did?"

"Oh, listen Jenny, you don't want to know."

"Maybe I do, Dad."

"Well, I wasn't too kind. In fact, I was downright rude."

"Did he try to give Christ the glory for his success?"

"Yeah, something like that."

"Have you ever thought about that? I mean God?" Jennifer knew she was pressing but also thought this was a good moment to complement Bell's words.

"Yeah, a long time ago," Jimmy said, feeling the heat rise under his collar. "But then I went away from God and the church. I was simply tired of all the rules and what you can do and what you can't do. Plus, I wanted to do what I wanted to do, and no one was going to tell me different."

She continued: "Well, did it work? Did you find happiness, or maybe success?"

"Success? Maybe some. I have a good job, and I really like what I'm doing. But happiness? I guess not. I mean, the single life isn't all it's cracked up to be . . . . Say, you seem to know a lot about all this religious stuff. Sort of like you know about baseball."

"Yes, something like that," she said. "I became a follower of Christ when I was 8 years old. The same year I started following baseball. Maybe you should give Him some thought."

Jimmy said he would, though the way he said it had a hollow ring to it that Jennifer could hear. Either way, he tried to laugh it off: "Don't tell those other writers; they'll start calling me Billy Sunday or Elmer Gantry or worse."

The name Sunday reminded Jennifer of the old-time ballplayer's final sermon before he died. She asked Jimmy, "Do you know what the title of that sermon was?"

"No, what?"

"He asked the question: 'What must I do to be saved?' "

"No kidding," Jimmy said with a hint of sarcasm. "Well what do you know about that?"

✱ ✱ ✱

The next day was an off-day for the team, and Jennifer and Jimmy had time to play tennis. It turns out that she was the No. 1 player for her high school team, and Jimmy did all he could to win the first set, 7-5. In the second set, Jennifer was easily leading, 5-1, when Jimmy was running toward the net and reached down to dig out a backhand volley. A sharp pain shot up through his left shoulder to his neck. The pain was so wrenching that it sent him to the concrete court, ending the match.

The pain wouldn't subside, and they decided Jimmy needed medical treatment. A chiropractor he knew applied ice to his back and adjusted his neck. Two colleagues came into the room to add their expertise, and together they tried a combination of manipulations to revive the loss of feeling in Jimmy's left thumb and forefinger. Although X-rays were inconclusive about any nerve damage at the C-6 and C-7 levels of the cervical portion of the spine, they did reveal one telling detail. There was no mistaking that Jimmy had a condition from birth that no one knew about until now. He had spondylolisthesis.

Dr. Morgan, the chiropractor, described the congenital condition as a defect of the wing-like parts on the vertebrae that hold the vertebrae in place. If the wing is missing or has been broken through some trauma, one vertebra can slip and press on the spinal cord or a nerve. "Yours is at the L-5 and S-1 levels of the spine," Dr. Morgan said. "That means the fifth level of the lumbar spine and the first level of the sacrum portion. This has nothing to do with the problem in your cervical part of the spine. Rather, you probably have some lower back pain."

"Some, yes," Jimmy said.

"And do you have any weakness in your legs?"

"Only some in my lower legs, the shin muscles, if I try to walk fast or over deep sand, like on a beach," Jimmy said. "But what about arm weakness?" He was thinking of his arm problem.

"It is possible there is a relationship," Dr. Morgan said. "Certainly, spondylolisthesis is seen in children who play sports."

"I can tell you that I rather suddenly lost strength in my throwing arm when I was 22," Jimmy said.

"Well, it usually shows up before that, but was there any trauma?" Dr. Morgan asked.

It was so long ago that Jimmy needed a moment to go back to that day when he and his teammate were running windsprints in the gym and Jimmy fell hard on his tail bone.

"When I fell," he said, "it was the usual pain that goes away in a few minutes. I didn't go to a doctor, and I just forgot about it . . . until now."

"It's difficult to conclude that that is what happened, and it is a congenital problem, so it may be that the fall was traumatic enough that it exacerbated the existing condition. Did you do anything else to injure your arm or shoulder?"

"No, nothing," Jimmy said. "And I always thought it was a problem with my shoulder. It seems that wasn't the problem at all."

Dr. Morgan agreed. "You're probably right."

His neck and back felt better, and Jimmy was ready to resume his daily workouts at home the next day.

✱ ✱ ✱

"Good morning, Dad. How are you feeling?" Jennifer asked as she came out of her bedroom.

"I'm doing fine, and the neck pain is much better. The chiropractors and the ice treatment did wonders. I'm going to start my usual workout."

After he rode 40 minutes on a stationary bicycle, he did 100 abdominal crunches and 50 modified squats with 10-pound weights in each hand. Then, he started to do pushups.

"Hey, wait a minute," Jennifer said. "Why are you doing pushups like girls do? On your knees? Why not do them like men?"

Jimmy had an answer that went back 20 years. "Ever since college, when I couldn't throw any more . . . well, I could throw but without any 'pop' . . . I found that I could NOT do pushups or pull-ups. I mean, I could do three or four of each, and then I would just lock up. I wasn't tired or weak, and nothing hurt. I simply could NOT move." He emphasized the word "not" and repeated it.

"OK, I understand," she said. "Would you be willing to try a man's pushup?"

"Sure. Here goes."

Suddenly it was as if special lubrication freed a frozen piston, and he was free. He easily popped off 20 pushups.

"Hey! This is fabulous! I'm going to try some pull-ups on the bar outside on the patio."

The magic was still working, and he ripped off 20 pull-ups in no time.

"Can you catch a ball?" he asked Jennifer. "Because I have an idea."

"Uh, I can catch, of course, but nothing too fast."

He dug out a hard ball and his fielder's glove from 20 years earlier. Finding the catcher's mitt that Norman's mother, Evelyn, gave him after he died took some digging through several boxes, first in the garage, next a bedroom closet and finally the hall closet. At last, there it was, hardly any worse for wear. For a moment, Jimmy feared the mitt was gone forever.

Jimmy and Jennifer stepped into the back yard, and he threw a couple of pitches softly to her. So far, so good. He stepped back a few feet and threw two more.

"Are you OK?" he called to her.

"Well, yes, but no harder."

"Let me call my neighbor. I think he'll be better. I don't want you to get hurt."

Dave, the neighbor, was able to come right over, and he grabbed the catcher's mitt. "Where in the world did you get this thing?" he asked. "It is ancient, and it has a tear in the pocket. And the web is missing some strings."

"Yeah, yeah, I know," Jimmy said. "But it will be OK for a few throws. If you're ready, just move back to near the fence. Yeah, right there. OK, I need to be back a little farther."

Jimmy threw two pitches easily and without pain. He warned Dave he was going to turn up the dial a little. Dave said he was ready. He squatted behind the imaginary home plate. Jimmy marked a place in the grass for an imaginary pitcher's rubber. Then, he threw a fastball with some heat. It surprised both of them, but mainly Dave. It was all he could do to catch the next pitch because of the sinking movement. Jennifer was standing off to the side and was startled by the hiss of the ball and the pop of the mitt. Jimmy decided he better turn down the dial, but he wanted to test his arm a little more.

"Dave, I'm going to throw a curve," he said. "I won't throw it hard. I'll just spin it." But even the soft curve broke more than Dave expected, and the ball disappeared under his glove, bounced and hit the fence.

Jimmy told Dave, "That's enough, but don't move from your position. I'm curious and want to measure the distance I was throwing from you to the hole in the grass where my right foot dragged." He went into the garage and came out with a tape measure. He asked Jennifer to put the tape measure on the back of the spot dug out in the grass, as he pulled out the tape all the way to Dave. It measured precisely 60 feet, 6 inches.

"Dad," she exclaimed, "that's the exact distance from the pitcher's rubber to home plate. How did you know that without measuring it first?"

Jimmy said, "I didn't know. It just came naturally."

"That's amazing," Dave said. "And your throws burned my hand. Well, through the old mitt."

"OK," Jimmy said, "but I need to do one more test. It'll have to wait until tomorrow afternoon when I can go out to the ballpark early."

As Jimmy put the glove, the mitt and the ball in the closet, Jennifer cleared her throat, wanting to say something important: "Dad, tomorrow is Sunday. Do you think we could find a church? I mean, I could skip a Sunday, but I really don't like to. So, what do you say?"

"Well, sure. You don't think the building will fall in on me, do you? I mean, it has been 22 years since I've been inside a church, except for a wedding or two, or a funeral."

"No, Dad, everything will be fine," she assured him.

In bed that night, Jimmy tossed and turned, and his mind churned. He couldn't relax because of the excitement about his ability to throw again, and that wasn't all. Jennifer's words kept nagging in his ear. Or was it something else? Or someone else? Jimmy had read stories about people who sometimes heard the voice of God, literally and out loud. This wasn't one of those times, but there was no doubt that these words formed very clearly in his mind: "Jimmy, years ago you had many opportunities to follow Me, and you were too afraid to do it. You thought it would be too restrictive, too confining, too churchy, if I may use that term, and you wanted to live your life the way you wanted. Well, you have and now here we are. My question to you: When are you going to get serious about Me?"

Jimmy didn't jump out of bed, fall on his knees and pray to ask God to come into his life and forgive him of his sins. Still, he knew at that moment he had made a commitment to God and to follow Christ the rest of his life. Indeed, he was a changed man.

He was itching to tell Jennifer but waited as they rode to church the next morning. "Something happened last night," he said. "God changed my life, and Christ came into my life."

Jennifer would have jumped for joy, but her seat belt kept her in the seat and in Jimmy's convertible, which had the top down. "That's wonderful, Dad. Tell me more about what happened."

"Well, I kept remembering your words, but I also remembered the first time I ever went to church. Our next-door neighbors took me. Not my parents. They never went to church. I was only 5 years old. It was a sunny spring day with white blossoms on the trees, I remember it clearly, and I remember hearing one song: 'Jesus loves me/This I know/For the Bible tells me so.' I remember feeling the loving arms of Jesus wrap around me as I climbed up into His lap. Hey, that's what 5-year-olds do. Through the years, in church, I had many opportunities to go forward, as they say, but it was like my butt was stuck in cement. I couldn't have moved if my life depended on it. Then, unfortunately, I went away from God until now. That was 22 years ago."

After a stirring church service of music and preaching, they stopped for a late lunch on the way to the ballpark.

Jimmy and Jennifer arrived while the Sacramento Solon team was taking batting practice. The grizzled manager, Clint "Jaws" Collins, was standing in front of the third base dugout. You couldn't miss him because he was a sight to behold. It was difficult to say who wore his uniform sloppier—him or Max Patkin, the Clown Prince of Baseball. Not only were his baseball pants bloused unevenly, Collins walked with a slight limp, a plug of tobacco made one cheek bulge like a goiter and his jaw was cocked to one side. His jaw was left that way after he took a line drive at third base in Cleveland in 1958, and why he was affectionately called "Jaws." There were rumors that he got it by jawing at umpires, but that wasn't true because he rarely was tossed out of a game. "My job is to manage, not get thrown out," he said. Or some people thought it was because of the Red Man tobacco he chewed. If that were true, he'd probably be called "Cheeks," and that conjures up something entirely different.

Nevertheless, Collins always had an obscene greeting for Jimmy, and this time was no different. "Here comes that fag sportswriter," he said and chuckled to let him know Jimmy was really OK in his book, even if Jimmy second-guessed his strategy from time to time in his game stories.

"Why didn't you have Jack King bunt?" Jimmy once asked. King was developing into a feared power hitter.

Jaws recognized King's raw talent and went out on a limb, which was rare for him. "That shows how much you know. If King hits in the Show like he's hitting at Triple A," Jaws predicted, "he'll be in the Hall of Fame by Friday. They don't need any bunters in the bigs." Then, he harrumphed off, barking over his shoulder to Jimmy: "You'd make a great manager in the flipping Japanese leagues." Of course he didn't really say "flipping."

Jaws claimed he never read anything, let alone the sports pages. "Why should I read you blowhards?" he asked. "You'd only tick me off. And anyway, I'm a baseball guy, and what do you know?" The truth was, Jaws read every author he could get his hands on, from Swift to Keats to Byron to Fitzgerald to Hemingway to Thurber, and almost everybody else in between. And certainly he read the daily box scores.

"Say, Jaws," Jimmy said this time, "I've got a special request."

"Oh, brother, now what?" Jaws said, feigning annoyance.

"Could I borrow one of your catchers for a while in the bullpen?"

"Sure, just as long as you don't screw up any of my players."

Jimmy took only a few throws to warm up in the valley heat. He was ready to cut loose and signaled fast ball to the catcher. He was throwing as hard as he had ever thrown 20 years earlier. And he was keeping the ball down at the knees. Within moments, other pitchers stopped their running and gathered around to watch. Most of them knew Jimmy, but one pitcher was new. He had been sent down on a rehabilitation assignment from the big league team.

"Who's the guy with the big league moss?" he said, looking at Jimmy's permed hair.

A teammate said, "He's a sportswriter."

"Gimme a break. Can't be."

"It's true. He covers our team."

"Well, sign him up. He's throwing around 90 miles an hour."

Jimmy said, "OK, that's enough for now." He was more than pleased and joked: "Not bad for a 42-year-old scribe."

Jimmy recalled that the Milwaukee Braves' Warren Spahn was the same age when he pitched 15⅓ innings of scoreless baseball against the San Francisco Giants in 1963. The Giants' 25-year-old Juan Marichal matched him inning for inning and refused to come out as long as the "old-timer" was still out there humping it up. In the bottom of the 16th inning, Spahn lost the game when Willie Mays hit a solo home run. Spahn ended that season with a 23-7 record at age 42. Jimmy knew darned well he wasn't in the same senior league.

Unseen by Jimmy, Jaws was watching out of the corner of his eye from his seat in the dugout. Jaws thought, "Heck, maybe he could throw in the Japanese leagues."

In the late innings that night, it was one of those rare times when Jaws got into a brouhaha with one of the worst umpires to reach Triple A, maybe ever. Jaws finally skulked back to the dugout. Then, pitches were thrown at heads, batters were drilled in the ribs and players charged from both dugouts. The two-umpire crew separated players as well as they could and were tossing pitchers, position players and many of the extra players out of the game. All but eight players on Jaws' entire roster had been kicked out of the game, and Jaws, too.

Jaws looked around and appointed Harry the trainer to run the team. "Hold everything," Jaws said. He saw they were one player short of fielding a team, and completely out of pitchers. What to do? Nothing like this had happened in Jaws' 45 years in the game. Although he knew the old chestnut about "something happens in baseball every day that you've never seen before," this was a fiasco. Sure, other position players had good arms, but pitch? Oh, some had fooled around with throwing knuckleballs. Playing around with knuckleballs has been a pastime for players since the days of Cap Anson, and Mickey Mantle supposedly threw a wicked knuckleball. But bring him in to pitch? It would add to the travesty, and in the thick of a pennant race, even if it was only Triple A. So, then, how not to forfeit the game?

Jaws told Harry, "Get him down here."

"Who?" Harry asked.

"The scribe."

Harry looked apoplectic, and his lower lip quivered and his eyes watered.

They turned toward the press box and pointed emphatically. It wasn't clear immediately what they wanted because there was a good distance between the field and press box, and then someone figured out they were motioning to Jimmy and Jaws was mouthing the words: "You, get down here. Yeah, you, the scribe." He wanted to enlist Jimmy as a fill-in player? Jimmy couldn't believe it, nobody in the stands could believe it and the play-by-play radio announcer was speechless.

For at least 15 years, Jimmy had covered this team, and there were good teams and bad. Especially with bad teams, inexplicable plays would happen, so Jimmy had to pay attention. There were other times when his mind would wander, and he would count the crowd of, perhaps, 674 people, or he sat in the sweltering press box playing a mind game of "what if?" What if the team ran out of players? What if someone got injured? What if they needed a fill-in player? Night after night, game after game, he secretly imagined that he would be called. It was strictly a figment of his imagination, and it amused him. He knew it never would happen, never could happen. But it was becoming reality . . . now. This was Walter Mitty at his loopiest.

"This can't be possible," Jimmy thought, silently protesting while the thrill of the idea ran through him. "I know it's an important game in the pennant race, but couldn't the game be suspended and resumed later with at least nine players?" Still, it was happening, and Jimmy was racing down to the clubhouse to change his clothes. Because he did work out with the team, his glove and spikes were waiting. His old uniform pants were hanging on a nail. There was no time to find a complete home town "uni," only a top with the words "Solons" on it.

While he was getting ready, Jaws and Harry conferred with the crew chief who agreed that, OK, though it was highly unusual, it was allowable. "But first," the umpire said, "he will have to sign a contract to make it official and legal with the league and minor league baseball." The major league team's general manager was making a rare visit to the team but watching with intense interest. When he saw what was about to happen—and definitely what was needed, he rushed to the field with a contract in his brief case. As Jimmy emerged from the tunnel and onto the field, the GM shoved a player contract into his hands and said: "Sign here." Jimmy did, and he was officially a Sacramento Solon and a professional baseball player at last.

Peace had been restored, and the umpire permitted Jaws to meet with Jimmy. "All right, Scribe," Jaws said as he handed Jimmy the ball, "listen carefully. They're gonna give you more time than usual to warm up, so take it easy. You'll know when you're loose. Go over the signs with Mike. He'll keep them simple. Nobody's out and a runner's on first. Don't worry so much about him. Get the batter. And remember, keep the ball down. I mean every pitch. Down. At the knees or below the strike zone. Pitch inside if you want, but don't hit anybody or we'll have World War Four on our hands. We've already had World War Three. Ya got it? Ready? Go get 'em, Meat."

Jimmy had gone from Scribe to Meat that quickly, and it must have helped him. He took a relaxing breath and let it out.

Understandably, he was a little nervous. It was a good nervousness, and, with it, there is an underlying foundation of confidence. If bad nervousness and luck are all you have, you'll get tattooed. Plus, he knew he had his arm back.

Still, this was his first game on the mound in two decades. He had watched a lot of young pitchers come through the league in that time—and Jimmy had imagined how he would pitch again—if he ever could. He'd abandon a windmill windup for a no windup. He'd pitch inside more and pound the outside corner. He'd add a four-seam fastball, not just a two-seamer. It would give his fastball a little more velocity. And he vowed to perfect a change-up. No one had ever taught him how to throw one. In fact, when he was growing up, no coach he had ever taught him any techniques: Either you could play or you couldn't. Fortunately, he could. The defining difference for him and his pals who could play was something they also came by as a matter of course: The more innings you could put under your belt, the better, and you would learn how to deal automatically with more situations. One of his coaches always said: "Know ahead of time the situation and what you'll do with the ball." When a player changed his mind mid-play, the coach would let everyone know: "You're thinking again." Of course, it helped if you played teams a little better than you and challenged you. Challenges were the ultimate teacher.

But this was no time to swing from the light towers with all those mental gymnastics. It was time to pitch. There was no stretching out cords in his forearm; there was no developing a callous on the forefinger or middle finger. Jimmy simply had to rely on the latent strength in his arm, back and leg muscles.

Jimmy's first challenge was the opposing catcher, Ed Swarthout. His face looked dark and menacing as if he'd just ended a shift at a steel mill where he carried steaming 100-pound bars in his bare hands, and wasn't too happy about it. When Swarthout gripped the bat, he left burn marks in the wood. Or so it seemed.

Jimmy figured Swarthout would be salivating at the sight of him, the emergency player. He'd be swinging and coming out of his shoes. The advantage would be Jimmy's. He had seen Swarthout and his teammates, but they hadn't seen him.

The first pitch: Ball one.

The second pitch: Ball two.

"Oh, oh, here we go again," Jimmy muttered. It was just like 20 years earlier. He was pitching backward again, needing to throw curve balls when behind in the count. Harry was getting nervous, and so was Jaws, hiding in the dugout tunnel but watching closely. "Bow your neck," he yelled. It was something players always said, and nobody had any idea what it meant.

The third pitch: Jimmy threw a slow curve that Swarthout missed by a foot.

The fourth pitch: An inside fastball, and Swarthout ramicackled it down the left-field line. Foul.

"OK," Jimmy told himself, "let's not do that again, so make sure you waste one, but don't make it an easy take." The four-seam fastball was outside by three inches. Now, if Swarthout missed a curve the first time, throw it again but throw an overhand curve with a straight-down break. And get it down, even bouncing it if necessary. Sure enough the ball short-hopped into the catcher's mitt as Swarthout chased the pitch and missed: Strike three.

The next batter was jammed and fisted a slow grounder to third base, and the Solons got only a force out at second base.

Two outs, top of the ninth, a one-run lead and another dangerous batter in the box. The batter was a veteran who had hit 100 home runs in his first three years in the big leagues. He had been sent down because of an injury, or so the story went. In reality, the player had a drinking problem, and the front office was tired of dealing with it and concocted the injury story. Quickly, Jimmy threw two strikes, first with another curve and then with a fastball the batter hit cattywampus down the left field line—again foul. So, Jimmy thought, challenge him again and find out how good my rediscovered fastball really is. But don't fool yourself and think you can throw it past him. Make it low on the outside corner. Jimmy had watched this guy before, and he could turn around a 95-mile-an-hour fastball and rake it down the left-field line as if it were a 60-mile-an-hour batting practice lob. With another deep breath, Jimmy let his best effort fly. The pitch was almost right where he wanted it, though it caught more of the plate than he intended—in fact, it was right down Broadway. The batter froze, guessing badly that Jimmy would throw a breaking pitch. Strike three! Game over!

His new teammates flooded the field to congratulate Jimmy as if he had just completed a 20-win season, while it was only his first appearance in 20 years. The other team could only sit stunned in the other dugout and watch—stymied by a temporary player, a sportswriter, for cryin' out loud.

Jimmy's two newspaper colleagues rushed into the clubhouse to greet the new hero and get the inside story.

Dirk Brown of *The Bee* reached him first. He blurted: "Jimmy, where did you learn to pitch like that? We never had any idea. Well, you told us you played in college, but this isn't college."

Jimmy said, "I know you want the inside story, just as I would, because we're all in the same business, but, first, I must tell you that I have to give all the glory to my Lord and Savior."

"Ah, now, Jimmy, c'mon. Cut out all that stuff," Brown pleaded. "We've heard it before and all about the God Squad. Now tell us about the game."

Sam Johnson of *The Union* had more incisive questions: "Jimmy, did you think you could throw the ball by the final batter? And what's next? Will they make you a starter? Or will you stay in the bullpen?"

"Well, guys," Jimmy said, "this might be a one-time appearance. Who knows? You'd better go ask Jaws."

Jaws played it cool and said, "The GM and I will have to talk about it. This certainly changes things. Of course we'd have to make room on the roster, and that means Jimmy would take somebody else's job. Either someone gets released or sent down. Somebody's not going to be too happy."

The decision was made to add Jimmy to the roster after the GM and the league office approved the move, clearly an unorthodox situation. One veteran player—the kind who was at the end of his career and simply hanging on—was made a coach, so he was able to stay with the team, at least for the next few games, depending on what Jimmy did. Even Jaws realized that this could be a one-time deal.

Two nights later, Jimmy came in, in long relief. In the fifth inning, he gave up a meaningless base hit and retired the side. In the sixth, he got three outs on a total of nine pitches. But then, in the seventh, he wanted to throw the lead-off batter his best fastball. It may as well have been an eephus pitch, like pitcher Rip Sewell's rainbow throw. The ball floated toward the catcher, Mike Sanders, and was hit for a towering home run. Jimmy had that sinking feeling that every pitcher instantly feels in his gut. He knows the ball is gone, it's not coming back and there's nothing he can do about it.

Echoing in his mind's ear, all the way back to 1951, Jimmy could hear Yankee announcer Mel Allen: "Going, going, gone! It's a Ballantine blast! How about that!"

Jimmy felt all right, but something had changed. On the next pitch, the same results: another floater, another home run, another Ballantine blast. "All right, Mel, you don't have to say a word," he thought.

Jaws rushed to the mound with catcher Sanders closed behind. "What's his ball doing, Mike?"

Sanders looked dumbfounded. "I don't know, Jaws. I haven't caught a pitch this inning."

Jimmy, though eager to continue, was realistic and spoke up: "Jaws, I think I've lost it again, just like 20 years ago. I'm throwing as hard as I can, and there's nothing on the ball."

"Yeah, so I've seen. OK, I'm taking you out. See Harry for a rubdown and we'll see how you feel tomorrow."

Tomorrow was no better. Jimmy thought he knew the magical answer: Go back to the chiropractor. He'll know what to do. Jimmy told the doctor what had happened and said, "Doc, whatever you did to fix the problem, do it again."

"Jimmy, I'd like to," Dr. Morgan said, "but I don't know what I did or what the other doctors did. It's a complete mystery."

As quick and simple as that, that was the end of Jimmy's short-lived baseball career.

"Well, it was great while it lasted," he told Jennifer.

"Dad, you were great . . . uh . . . until that second game."

"You are right. It was fun to be able to throw again, if only for a while. I can't understand why the chiropractors couldn't fix it again. At least now we know there was never anything wrong with my shoulder, or rotator cuff. That's what everyone thought at first. Well, Jennifer, what are your plans now that you've found your dad, met a grizzled sportswriter and watched a sore-armed pitcher go from girls' pushups to success and back to failure?"

"Please, Dad, it wasn't that bad. In fact, my dream came true . . . for you, too. We found out a lot about each other, and I'm glad we connected and have a lot in common. We both went back a long ways. I found you, and you found your spiritual roots again."

"I guess, no, I know, I owe a lot to you for coming back to God."

✳ ✳ ✳

After Jennifer returned home to Phoenix, they exchanged phone calls regularly and notes and cards, especially on their birthdays, and met in either Phoenix or Sacramento once or twice a year. Eleven years had passed since their first reunion, and Jennifer thought they needed a special occasion to celebrate it. She had an idea that she knew Jimmy would like.

"Hi, Dad," she said during a phone call to Oakville.

"Hi, Jenny," he said. "But this isn't your normal time to call me."

"I know," she said. "I think we should meet, and I have an idea."

"OK, I give. Shoot," he said.

"Well, let's meet halfway between Oakville and Phoenix."

"And where would that be?"

"In Los Angeles at Dodger Stadium," she said. "It's the final game of the regular season, and the Giants need to win. If they do, then there would be a playoff."

"Yeah, I know," he said, "and the Giants are starting a rookie pitcher. Of course he's all they have left." They were forced to use their two best starters to even get a shot at a playoff.

She caught on, and said: "Well, maybe you could get your arm massaged and . . . ."

"No, no," he objected and chuckled: "That fantasy is all behind me."

Jimmy arranged for two tickets to the game and bought Jennifer a plane ticket to Los Angeles. He drove down from Oakville and picked her up at the Burbank airport the morning of the game. They arrived at Dodger Stadium early because they wanted to watch both teams take batting practice. The season had had a classic pennant race of its own, and, although the Dodgers were far out of the running, the Giants and Dodgers were going head to head, as usual in their 104-year-long rivalry. The Giants would play the Braves in a one-game playoff if they won, and who better to be the spoiler than their rivals, the hated Dodgers?

As they walked along the Dodger Stadium concourse on the way to their seats, Jimmy stopped so abruptly that Jennifer thought there was something wrong. Jimmy's face had a ghostly look.

Jimmy had never seen Bobby Thomson play, either before the 1951 season or later, because major league baseball—namely the Giants and the Dodgers—hadn't yet forsaken New York for the West Coast. The TV Game of the Week, announced by Dizzy Dean and Buddy Blattner, came along in 1954. Jimmy's dad finally bought a TV in 1955.

As Jimmy and Jennifer stopped cold, unmistakably, without the shadow of a doubt, there was Bobby Thomson, as big as life, talking with a front-office official for the Giants, and smiling as happily as the newswire photos showed him being mobbed by teammates after his "Shot Heard 'Round the World" in 1951. He gladly interrupted his conversation to say hello to Jimmy and Jennifer, total strangers, and Jimmy took his picture.

Four hours later, a mediocre Dodger team had pummeled the Giants, 12-1, and left them walking, single file, disconsolately through long shadows, to a gate in centerfield and beyond to the team bus. The Dodgers made certain there would be no Giants dancing victoriously in their Cathedral of Baseball, Dodger Stadium. There would be no latter-day replay of the Miracle of Coogan's Bluff—or Chavez Ravine, in this case—and certainly no joy for Giant fans. It was October 3, 1993, exactly 42 years after Thomson's home run. Despite 103 wins, the Giants had lost the pennant.

Epilogue

When Jimmy drove to Southern California to meet Jennifer, he zipped past Marshfield, and it occurred to him that he should make a point of stopping to see what the Original Edison Field looked like so many years later. After all, it's only a two-hour drive from Oakville. Somehow, he never seemed to be able to find the time, and the years flew by.

Then, Bobby Thomson died, two months before the Giants won their first World Series in San Francisco, in 2010, and he knew he had to do it, but he wanted the time to be special. He decided it would be the next spring—exactly 60 years after the birth of the Original Edison Field.

On a blustery March day, much like the one when Norman came out and asked whether he could join in a game of catch, Jimmy took the Main Street exit off the freeway and turned onto Edison Street. Three short blocks later, he pulled slowly up in front of 406 E. Edison St.

As he surveyed the surrounding landscape, Jimmy scarcely recognized the old place there were so many changes.

The street was a wide, smooth thoroughfare, with curbs and gutters. A housing tract had replaced the pasture on the north side. The tangled honeysuckle bush was long gone, and the 4-foot-high hedge that served as the outfield wall had been replaced by a wrought-iron fence with climbing roses. It surrounded three-quarters of the lawn, separating it from the driveway at Norman's house. The fence had a gate closing off "Home Run Alley." Only one of the two magnolia trees remained. They spread so wide that Jimmy assumed there was room enough for only one. The evergreen bush, where Norman placed his walker and pitched, also was missing. But the S-curved sidewalk was the same as always, and, from a distance, he could make out the crack that a batted ball had to cross. White siding made the house look almost new. Still, there was no getting around it: The house was in its seventh decade.

After a moment or two passed, Jimmy's old front yard looked as fresh as ever. It had changed; that's all. The memories never would.

Would he dare get out of his car and go up to the front door and knock and explain to the strangers who lived there who he was and how their lawn was a healing place for a 10-year-old boy, and Norman, too? He resisted the urge and decided to leave that time just as it was.

Bobby Thomson
Oct. 25, 1923 – Aug. 16, 2010